What the Good Girl Knew

L. B. ANNE

JOA PRESS
FLORIDA

For information, Address JOA Press

P.O. Box 7984, Seminole, Florida 33775.

www.joapress.com

Cover art © 2024 by Miss Vie Book Designs

Edited by Samantha Mendell

Library of Congress Control Number: 2024919722

ISBN 979-8-9889776-2-9

What the Good Girl Knew

Other books by L. B. Anne:

Never Really Gone

The Sheena Meyer Series:
The Girl Who Looked Beyond the Stars
The Girl Who Spoke to the Wind
The Girl Who Captured the Sun
The Girl Who Became a Warrior
City of Gleamers
Secret of Shadow and Light
May Your Vision Be True
Fate of the Gleam Keeper

Knights of the Gleam Series:
Angel Girl Awakening
Hidden Thorns

Everfall Series:
Before I Let Go
If I Fail
All the Scars

Storm's truth will change everything

1

A heavy sigh slipped from my lips as I reread the warning, then flopped back onto my bed. "Ugh. Why me, God?"

Beacon High's administrators might see this project as some kind of rite of passage, a last-ditch effort to make us "real-world ready," but for me, it was nothing but a sick joke. I skimmed through the PDF they sent to the entire senior class.

There it was, in bold, soul-crushing letters: **Senior Project**. The unavoidable hurdle standing between me and graduation.

"'Failure to complete the project will mean the student will not be eligible to graduate in May. If any one of these components of the Senior Project receives an unsatisfactory evaluation, the student must rectify the situation before receiving a Beacon High School diploma.'

"Seriously? Beacon High will hold my diploma hostage?" No pressure or anything. But failing? Not an option. So, I flung myself upright, grabbed my pen, and started writing:

Who am I? That's like the ultimate existential crisis right there. It's a question I've asked myself more times than I care to admit. It keeps me up at night, along with thoughts of whether bacon belongs on a peanut butter sandwich or how tall Jesus was. People were shorter back then, so I wonder—was he as tall as me? Anyway, In the shadows of a dream, a voice once claimed, "You were birthed from a storm." It was true—hence the reason my mother loved to share the story with strangers. And by "strangers", I mean the cashier at the Piggly Wiggly, the barista at the Cocoa Bean, or anyone who made eye contact for longer than three seconds. "This is my daughter. She's a walking natural disaster," I mouth verbatim as she says it. My mom doesn't mean it in a bad way, she is just a little out of touch with what's actually funny. It's cool though. I do have an unbelievable origin story. My mother likes to add dramatic emphasis—sound effects and all—when she tells it, reenacting the loud booms of thunder and bright flashes of lightning that accompanied my arrival into this world. To her credit, she definitely makes it a memorable story. But it wasn't like I had any control over when and where I entered the world, as if I could have waited for a sunny day with a slight breeze and birds chirping. Nope, I made my dramatic entrance during one of Mother Nature's most intense displays of power.

I stared at the page, tapping my pen lightly on the edge of my notebook, wondering how much detail would impress Mrs. Caplan. I could already hear her saying, "Show, don't tell." The words repeated in my head, so with a sigh, I pressed the pen back to the paper—hard enough to puncture it—and continued writing:

The streets were a mess. Storm water spilled over the curbs, and downed trees blocked what little path remained. Rain hammered the windshield of my mother's car in relentless sheets, making it nearly impossible for her to see. She winced as another contraction gripped her, slamming on the brakes in the middle of the flooded road, and put the car in park. With one hand on her belly, she stumbled out into the torrential rain, her breath shallow, her face pale as another contraction hit. She waved frantically at the blurred shapes of cars zooming by, begging for one—just one—to stop. A beat-up truck slowed and came to a stop. The driver stepped out, immediately drenched from the downpour as he approached her, rain running down his face and from his long dreadlocks. My mother looked into his eyes, which softened as he took in her condition. Without a word, he rushed to her side, helping her into his truck. She later found that he had lost his wife during childbirth just a few months prior. I was born right there in that truck. It even made the news. And thus my name: Storm. Honestly, can you imagine being named after a violent disturbance of the atmosphere? I've been thoroughly obsessed with weather since I was a kid. It's kind of my thing. At the drop of a hat, I can rattle off twenty benefits of storms: they bring rain, which we need; they break up clusters of harmful bacteria in stagnant water—yuck; they balance temperatures; they bring new life via seeds . . . You get the picture.

I tapped my pen against my lips. Okay, what else. I glanced out of my window. "Oh, I know . . ." I grinned. My brain was actually working with me, instead of doing that thing where it glitches and gives me random information I'm not looking for at the moment. After scribbling down the next part, I leaned back against my pillows and read it out loud.

"But in a small town like Spencer, where dirt roads outnumber paved ones, and Sunday sermons are heard amid the rustling of the oak trees that tower over backyard barbecues, I stand out like lightning on a clear day. I'm a living, breathing manifestation of the weather patterns that sweep across our quaint community. I can be mild and beautiful, embodying the gentle warmth of a sunlit afternoon that bathes the churchyard behind my house in golden hues. Yet, within me, there simmers the potential for a tempest, a turbulent force ready to unleash its wrath. It is a conflict I wrestle with daily, a choice between being chill or succumbing to the storm within.

"As a church girl, the expectation to embody goodness is ingrained, and I work diligently at it, even when the temptation to break free from the mold and elbow a classmate in the throat lingers beneath the surface of my composed exterior.

"Somehow, I developed this crazy idea that every storm that hit our city was my fault. My best friend, Kendra Medina, once grabbed me while I was in the middle of an all-out, snot-fest meltdown—tears flowing and snot dripping.

"'Storm, the hurricane isn't coming to Spencer because of you. Georgia is in its path. That's all,' she'd told me.

"But I never quite believed that was true.

"The hurricane-turned-tropical storm that threatened to tear my house apart mirrored what was happening inside me, constricting my airways, its path and intensity unpredictable. My breaths grew faster, and my chest rose and fell in desperate movements, trying to fill my lungs with air.

"My mother didn't bother with an ambulance. Kendra cradled my head in her lap in the backseat of Betty, our old sedan, and whispered, 'We've been here before. You've got this. You're going to be okay.'

"Before I knew it, arms grabbed me and carried me into the emergency room as my mother screamed for help. The rest of the memory is a blur of bronchodilators and systemic corticosteroids . . ."

I stopped reading and slammed my pen down on the worn page of my notebook, glaring at the words. "This is garbage. Why did I say, 'my arrival,' as if I'm writing a science fiction story about arriving from a space station on Titan? Sheesh."

Although I didn't think getting a C on the paper would affect my overall grade average much, I couldn't take that chance so close to the end of senior year.

My teeth sank into my lower lip as, for a moment, I considered fusing my story with the events of my father's passing to add a little raw emotion. Unlike my peers, I had no family history to write about for this project, so I chose to write my own.

"Stormie!"

"Ma'am?" That's how all the kids in Spencer were taught to respond to their mothers from a young age, unless they wanted a tap on their bottom.

"What are you doing? The food is hardening on these dishes."

"Homework! Why do we have a dishwasher when you always make me hand wash the dishes?"

My mother's feet thumped up the stairs. "You've asked me that a million times, and the answer is still the same: because we're saving water."

"Actually, studies have shown that we use up to twenty-seven gallons of water washing by hand and only about three gallons with an ENERGY STAR-rated dishwasher like ours."

"Why do you know that?" my mother asked as she barged into my bedroom. She wore her "mom uniform"—patterned leggings and an oversized t-shirt, hiding the belly she insisted she was still trying to lose from my birth sixteen years ago.

"Are you almost done? You've already been accepted to Florida State. Why are they still making you do homework?"

I laughed. "The school year is far from over, Mom. There's this little thing called a diploma that I still have to get."

"Yeah, but—Stormie . . ." She came close to my bed and stared at the V-neck of my jersey, watching me breathe. "Are you wheezing?"

"No, Mom. I'm okay. Please don't hover."

She lifted her hands, the tips of her fingers red from her evening snack of pomegranate arils, backed up, and spun away. Her blonde ponytail swung like a pendulum slicing through the air as she hurried over to the window to turn on the air purifier below it, then left the room. Its whir, like white noise, provided a rhythmic backdrop that I found relaxing, so I didn't complain about her turning it on this time.

"Let's do Pilates later," she called over her shoulder.

"I'm in." This week it was Pilates, next week it would be some other exercise regimen from a video that had gone viral on social media.

"Ooh!" she exclaimed. My eyes followed her head as she bobbed down the stairs on the other side of the rail. "Your father loved this song."

I sat upright, a sudden jolt coursing through me. *Did she just mention my father? The first time after, what has it been, almost four years?* I hopped up, glanced back at the notebook, then darted out of my room. Homework could wait.

When I got to the bottom of the stairs, I stopped and watched her shuffle back and forth in front of the coffee table. She wiggled her hips, completely oblivious to her lack of rhythm, but I wasn't going to be the one to tell her.

The last rays of daylight shone through the front window of the living room, stopping on the back wall adorned with artwork—mostly mine—as if to say, "That's it, girls, I'm off work in fifteen minutes. You'll have to deal with whatever the moon gives you after that." Which was a problem because my mother used no more lights than was necessary.

I approached and mirrored her every awkward step, trying not to burst out laughing. She grinned at me and cranked up the volume. Side to side we swayed over the large floor tiles, locked in a dance that compelled her to close her eyes and tilt her head, disappearing to another place.

Moments later, her eyes fluttered open, returning from wherever that special song had taken her.

"Was this his favorite?" I asked as she grabbed my hand and twirled me in front of her.

My mother's gaze met mine, briefly. Her grin vanished. She released my hand, reached for the volume control button on her phone, and turned it down. Then she picked up her water bottle from the coffee table, her hand shaking ever so slightly, and took a long sip. It was the care with which she set it back down that worried me.

"Mom, are you okay? Was that triggering? I'm sorry. You don't have to talk about him."

She shook her head as if shaking every thought from it. "It's okay. I'm sorry, I just can't discuss it."

"One day?"

"One day," she replied and walked away.

Pfft, one day? More like never. I scoffed inside.

My mind said "homework", but my feet were set on a different path. When it came to making decisions, I often trusted my feet over my brain, and it was usually a bad idea. For the moment, my feet wouldn't release me from that spot.

At sixteen, I was as empathetic as I could be, but my mother still wouldn't open up about my father. There were no traces of him in our home, no photos or mementos to help me piece together his life. In fact, there were no photos of anyone, except us. All that I knew about my father was that he was deceased—perished in a brutal battle tank explosion right before my mother's eyes during their military service. The memory still haunted her after so many years.

You don't know what that's like, I told myself. *I mean, hello? Loving someone and then watching them die right in front of you? That's enough to make anyone go bonkers. You can't even begin to imagine how she feels, so cut her some slack and give her all the time she needs. PTSD is no joke.*

For most of my life, my father was just a name on my birth certificate, but lately, I felt a deep ache inside for some connection to him. I craved to know details about his life, to fill in the missing gaps in my own. Did I inherit his sense of humor or his quirkiness? Was he smart too? What about his parents?

The house was silent as I listened for my mother's muffled sobs. There were none this time. That was a good sign that she wouldn't fall into another bout of depression.

From the coffee table, her cell phone called to me, beckoning me to pick it up. *Okay, I will.* It wasn't about spying; it was just an earnest desire to understand. My fingers gently traced the familiar pattern she used to unlock her screen. The phone lit up, and a music streaming app showed a list of songs.

There it was. Highlighted right below "I Will Survive" by Gloria Gaynor. I set her phone down and quietly retreated to my bedroom.

The air purifier hummed and blew, making the sheer curtains flutter away from the window. I snatched my notebook from my bed and sat at my desk, all the while imagining what it would be like to have a father. To have someone to cook with, like Kendra did with her dad. *Yeah, he would make the bomb vegan grilled cheese.* Or someone who would cheer me on at soccer games—or any sport, if I played sports. He would be so loud on the sidelines, just shy of embarrassing. *That would be kind of cool.*

But mostly, I just imagined someone with green eyes like mine, who would love me as much as my mother did—and that's saying something—despite my obsession with platform sneakers and kid goats.

"I should totally write about that. All right, enough melodrama. Time to get my senior year game face on." Nothing would stop me from finishing out my senior year strong, even though I was already graduating a year early.

Yet, as I delved into my notes and started typing them on my laptop, my thoughts gravitated back to that song. I couldn't help but feel frustrated. Why couldn't she just talk about him? Had he been on some top-secret CIA mission or something? Would I be in danger if I found out the truth about him?

That's it! We're in a witness protection program! I jotted it down. Even if it wasn't true, it might make my story more interesting.

To block out the noise in my head, I plugged in my headphones, and for the rest of the evening, I listened to the song my father had loved. The R&B melody was a supportive backdrop to my homework—the closest I had ever gotten to anything related to him.

Maybe it was the leftover pizza I had for dinner or that I finished off a bag of gummy bears before bed. More likely, though, it was the weight of those unresolved thoughts about my father that triggered the dream that night—the dream that would set the stage for the storm defining my reality.

2

My screams tore through the quiet hours of the morning, a haunting echo of the cryptic message that clung to my consciousness in a lingering whisper.

"'Who are you?' I had asked.

'I am your father,' the voice said. Not like Darth Vader in Star Wars, but in a low and gentle tone. He sounded more like the actor, Chadwick Boseman—may he rest in peace. His words were accompanied by visions of a clear sky marred by approaching thick gray clouds.

'My father? That's not possible.' I told him. 'What do you want?'

'To tell you of what is to come.' And that's when he told me the date . . . of the end."

"What did he look like?" my mom asked, brushing strands of hair from my face. She had heard my cries and came rushing into my room, looking frazzled and wielding a hammer over her head.

"I don't know. I didn't see him close enough. But—"

"Stormie, it was just a dream. It has no meaning."

"But he gave me a date."

"And what is it?"

My planner rested on my nightstand. I grabbed it and flipped the pages until I found June's calendar. "The same day as my graduation."

"See? This is what I'm talking about." She lifted my chin. "This dream is about what's going on inside of you regarding graduating from high school this year. It's not about the end of the world."

"You think so?"

"I am certain of it." She lifted the covers and slid into bed beside me, enveloping me in a warm hug.

I welcomed her embrace and leaned against her, breathing in the scent of honey lavender from her body wash and nuzzling into her soft sherpa robe.

"You're a good girl, Stormie. God wouldn't lay something that heavy on you. Plus, the Bible says no one knows when the end is." She kissed my forehead. "Are you feeling okay? You're a little warm."

"Maybe because I was screaming a moment ago?"

"Okay, that's true," she said and then went on about how I might be a little worried about going off to college and my health, and how I'm under so much stress. I listened to her until my eyelids grew heavy and her words became a hum.

It was just a dream, albeit a very vivid dream, unlike any I had ever had. And for that reason, the next day at school, I sat through my classes, ignoring the lessons.

In calculus, while my teacher discussed differential equations, I couldn't help but think, *What if when he said "your father," he didn't mean my biological father, but God himself? Like a divine paternity test or something. It would make sense with how he knew the exact date. But why me? Why would God reveal that to a sixteen-year-old nobody from a small town in Georgia?*

Lunch period at Beacon High was always a mad rush as my classmates scattered about the cafeteria, trying to find a seat with their friends. I grabbed a tray, went through the assembly line for my food, found a table, and pulled my composition book—aka my "brain dump" journal—out of my bag.

Everything I had seen and heard in the dream was still as clear as when I awoke. I wrote down the signs I was told would lead to the end of the world. The "signs" were more like a mash-up of things from an apocalypse movie and a conspiracy theory—definitely not the biblical version. But I couldn't dismiss them as just ramblings from a dream, even though some studies had shown that heavy meals before bed could trigger increased brain waves.

1. *The Crimson Star Ascends*

2. *The Heavens Weep*

3. *Gravity Unshackled*

4. *The Writhing Plague*

5. *The Day of Reckoning*

6. *The Dead Walk Among Us*

7. *The Final Dawn*

Staring at what I had written, I realized the signs made no sense at all. I rubbed my forehead and shook my head, embarrassed for thinking it was more than a dream.

"Storm!" Kendra spotted me and practically skipped over with her lunch tray. As she sat beside me, I closed my notebook.

"Saw that. What are you hiding?"

I lifted slightly from my seat and slid the notebook under my bottom, in case she tried to snatch it from me. "Nothing. This is a school. We have schoolwork."

"Oh, don't act like I don't know you better than anybody, Storm. And the fact that you chose to sit on the notebook, like a child, means it *is* something."

"All right, but it's nothing that I'm ready to share yet. How's that?"

"I'll take it, because I'm patient. You'll tell me. Eventually. You always do," Kendra replied and removed her cropped jean jacket adorned with Puerto Rico's flag on the back.

I skimmed her tray.

"Want half?" she asked, holding up her sub.

"You know I can't do dairy." I pointed at my face. "Serial mucus producer here."

"Yeah, sorry about that. I don't know what I would do if I couldn't eat ice cream."

"There are alternatives, you know? Plant based, sorbet..."

"Yeah, but still."

The cafeteria was a battlefield of voices. Each table, its own faction, alliances built over four years. And for many students, this chaotic lunch period was the highlight of their day. One of them being me, because I got to hang out with my best friend, unfiltered, without a parent around.

Most of my fellow seniors mingled with other tables or displayed their strong dislike for them. I prided myself on my neutrality and ability to get along with everyone—even the jocks and varsity dance girls, who mostly ignored anyone who wasn't part of their team. As far as I knew, most people genuinely liked me or perhaps they just pitied me because I was the "sick girl".

Kendra nodded toward the boy at the loudest table. "Pool is looking over here."

"What for?" I asked, scooping up a bit of peanut butter with a potato chip.

"Probably because you're doing something gross," Kendra replied and laughed.

"No worse than you eating ice cream with tortilla chips."

"Oh shoot, he's coming over," said Kendra. "I would clear my whole roster for him."

"What roster?"

"Pfft . . . You know I've got options. Okay, act natural. Everybody stay calm."

By everybody, she meant her.

"Puberty really did its thing on him, didn't it? How's my nose? Any boogers?"

"You're good," I reassured her, pretending to inspect her nostrils. Kendra had crushed on Pool for years, but he was always taken, and there were always more swooning girls ready to pounce at any moment.

"Hey, Storm." His thick brows lifted quickly and rested above his startling blue eyes.

"Chantler." I preferred to call him by his last name.

"What it do?" said Kendra. "Why did I say that?" she whispered.

"The seniors are hanging out at Okefenokee tomorrow night."

"The swamp?" asked Kendra.

"Oh, umm . . . yeah." He scratched his head. "So, are you in?" He placed his hands in the front pockets of his jeans and rocked on his heels.

I pointed at myself. "Me? No, I don't think so."

The chatter around us turned to a sudden hush, like someone had hit the mute button on a remote. Everyone in earshot looked over their shoulders, watching Pool.

Kendra's jaw practically dropped to the floor, her eyes fixed on his bulging biceps, visible even under his oversized T-shirt.

He plopped his left butt cheek on the table, way too close for comfort, and looked like he was trying to nail some cheesy stock photo pose. "Have you attended one senior party this year?"

"No, and there's a reason for that," I replied.

Pool and his "fan club" were notorious troublemakers. I had only heard rumors about their shenanigans outside of school. How does one decide to glue someone's car doors shut? And after having some kind of reaction to a bottle of nail polish remover, Neil still has a constellation of bumps across his hairline from using it to scrub off the words someone had written across his face with a Sharpie. Then, there was the incident with the black racer snake.

No, I definitely wasn't trying to become a part of some mess. Judging by how interested everyone was in the conversation, it was clear that there was some big secret I wasn't privy to.

"Oh, you're just going to put us on blast like that?" asked Pool. "Okay." He gave me his most charming grin. "We're cool, right?"

"Of course."

"Good." He pointed at me as he stood. "Reconsider. We'll be meeting up at the Okefenokee entrance around 8 p.m.," he said with a wink, then walked back to his table. As soon as he sat, Tiffany Lancaster flipped her hair extensions, draped her arm around him, and whispered in his ear.

"Sheesh, give him room to breathe," said Kendra. "She acts like they're in a rom-com or something . . . Was that her tongue?"

"Hey, I'm trying to eat here. I don't want to hear about her tongue or anyone else's. Not my circus, not my monkeys."

Kendra giggled. "What's that supposed to mean?"

"My mom says that. It means it's none of my business."

"Whatever, so what do you think that was about?" She twirled her braids around her finger while staring at Pool as if she were waiting for him to ask her to marry him.

"I have no idea. Why would they suddenly want to include me after basically ignoring me all these years?"

"Storm!" Kendra exclaimed, slapped her hands down on her lap, and leaned toward me. "You seriously don't know? Have you even looked in the mirror recently? This year?"

"I have no idea what you're talking about."

"Seriously, Storm, you have a killer figure. Thank your genetics because you don't do anything athletic—"

"I swim."

"Doesn't count."

"Clearly you know nothing about swimming and ought to join me once in a while."

"I don't even know what language you're speaking right now. Anyway, as I was saying, you have this natural tan, even in the dead of winter, thick hair that you always blow out but I keep telling you to leave curly. And your green eyes . . . You're driving all the boys crazy."

I rolled my eyes.

"You're lucky I'm a junior. I would've met up with them and dragged you along with me."

I side-eyed Pool's table and shook my head in disbelief. A boy stood up and shouted, "Nincompoop!", sending everyone in throes of laughter.

"Seriously? The swamp? I'm not buying it. Okefenokee closes at 6:30. What are they *really* planning?"

3

The bell rang and we exited the last class of the day as if someone had announced, "Free Takis!" Because, to be honest, we were always hungry and heading straight for the vending machines.

Asher strolled past me with a, "What's up, Storm." I gave him a grin in return and realized he hadn't been in class. I envied those who could skip school without a care in the world. I tried to once, during my rebellious stint, but my anxiety over getting caught put an end to that. Plus, missing calculus would only lead to failing exams, which meant failing grades and then goodbye college dreams. So, no thanks.

I sized Asher up: no belt, shoes untied, but his hair as neat as always. He could be a potential prom date, although he had never shown that type of interest in me.

I continued down the hall, past the media center, and was halfway to the exit door—so close to freedom—when Teresa Shinley sprung up in front of me like she had dropped from the sky rather than darted out of a classroom. We weren't exactly BFFs, but we had been friends for years. We met at church and became close because of our obsession with collecting Polly Pockets, even though they were discontinued. Teresa was kind and the only kid to attempt to get me help when I had one of my attacks.

"OMG, Storm!" she shrieked. Her boobs practically smacked me in the face before the rest of her body caught up. I couldn't help but think she purposely wore tight tops to show them off. Why did her parents let her out of the house like that?

"Are you going?" she asked with a happy bounce.

"Going where?"

"To hang out with Pool and, you know, everybody."

"They invited you too? I guess it's legit then."

"What do you mean by that?"

"Nothing. I just wasn't sure that was really happening."

"So you're coming?" she asked again, hopeful.

"Hard pass on *that* invitation. But text me afterward with all the juicy details."

Suddenly, a locker slammed shut and we both jumped.

Pool doubled over laughing, then ran toward us. "You should've seen your faces! Priceless!"

I placed my hand over my heart. "You play too much, Chantler."

He casually draped his arm around Teresa, who blushed and beamed. "Did you change your mind, Storm? T-Baby's coming."

T-Baby?

"Didn't she tell you?" He didn't look at me as he spoke. The top button of Teresa's shirt had come undone, and Pool's gaze lingered a moment too long, as if her breasts were talking to him instead of me.

"Nope, still not going. But have fun doing whatever it is you do at night in a closed swamp."

Pool's head snapped toward me. I grinned innocently, then turned and walked away. My exit was almost flawless. A witty remark and I was out, like a total boss.

But of course, it would be just my luck to nearly crash into a boy with an impressive head of curly hair. I awkwardly dodged him and muttered an apology before scurrying away, mentally adding yet another embarrassing moment to my ever-growing list. He gave me a curious look before continuing down the hall with an exaggerated swagger.

I made a beeline for the exit, trying to escape the buzz of excitement about the swamp hangout that filled the senior hall. Over the slamming of lockers I caught snippets of conversations:

"Apparently they're bringing fireworks."

"Dude, did you hear about the weird thing they found out there last time?"

"Ugh, Pool invited me, but I'm lowkey stressed about what to wear to a swamp party."

My phone chirped with a text from Kendra: *You're seriously not going? I hear it's going to be the party of the century!*

I snorted at her use of "the century" and replied: *Swamps and I don't vibe. Allergies, remember? Teresa is going and coming back with the deets. We'll see if she survives the night.*

The security officer saluted me—the final step of making it through the packed hallway—and I emerged onto the grid, a.k.a. the school parking lot. The grid was packed, and the car line was backed up for almost a mile. The city of Spencer was growing like crazy, yet still had just one high school.

Like me, most students at Beacon High had one mission: weave through the cars and escape school grounds ASAP. But just as I was about to reach my mom's car, my phone lit up with another text from Kendra. I couldn't wait to see what absurd tactic she would use this time to try to persuade me into going to the swamp.

What do you have against swamps?

The text wasn't from Kendra, but from a random number.
Me: *Umm . . . Who is this?*
Just a fellow senior.
Me: *Right, but what's your name?*

Not telling. Just answer the question.

I was intrigued about how this "fellow senior" got my number. Clearly, it was a boy because a girl wouldn't be so mysterious.

I texted back: *Nothing, really. Just not a fan of pollen, mosquitoes, and mysterious creatures lurking in the dark.*

Ha! Fair enough. Let's start a club for anti-swamp people. Or we can be team-antisocial together.

I giggled.

"What's so funny?" my mom asked as I climbed into the car and closed the door, still glued to my phone.

"Just some random person texting me about swamps," I said with a smile.

"Weird," she replied.

We should hang.

Me: *Why would I do that?*

To vent about the absurdity of high school parties in swamps, obviously.

I couldn't help but laugh.

"Now you *have* to tell me," she said. "I don't think I've ever seen you giggle so much. It's a boy, isn't it?"

Me: *Who are you?*

You'll find out soon enough. See you at school.

4

—·—

The car's A/C vents blew the sterile scent of hospital disinfectant at my face as Betty's engine shuddered to life. Mom was determined never to take on a car loan again, so we were stuck with Betty until Mom could either save up enough cash to buy a car outright or Betty finally broke down with no hope for repair.

But Betty was a fighter. At this rate, I'd probably be driving a spaceship before we got rid of the old clunker.

"Spill, Stormie. Don't keep me in suspense. What was that about?"

"You know, rideshare drivers are not supposed to be in their passenger's business."

"Oh, so now I'm your rideshare driver?"

With expert precision, she reached behind her back and unhooked her bra under her scrubs, then let out a sigh of relief. "Ah . . . that's so much better."

"Seriously, Mom? Can you not do that while driving?"

She shrugged nonchalantly and placed her attention back on the road. "Hey, I'm just trying to get comfortable for this long journey home."

"Oh yes, the very long and arduous one-mile drive. Now I'll have to add that to your review. And no tip." I laughed. "You do pick me up from school every single day like a hired driver."

"It's on my way home from work. Stop being silly."

My mother might not admit it, but she planned her work schedule around me. That way, she would know if I was lying about feeling fine after school and she could hover—her favorite thing to do where I was concerned.

"Back to the important question. Who was that person you were talking to?"

"I wish I had an answer for you, Mother Dear, but I don't. I have no idea who he is."

"What do you mean you don't know who he is?" she asked as we pulled into our driveway.

"It's true. You saw the whole text exchange."

She raised a skeptical brow. "But you laughed."

"That's what normal people do when others text funny things," I replied, opening the car door and getting out.

"He could be a stalker."

"Mom, please don't," I groaned.

"Please don't what?"

"Mom, would you get out of the car?"

She grabbed her purse out of the backseat and stepped out of the car as if her body weighed a ton. From the corner of my eye, I noticed her laser-focused stare burning holes into me as we trudged toward the front door. *Here we go*, I thought. *Here comes the lecture.*

To my mother, it wasn't an innocent text from a classmate, but from someone who should be on a Dateline news show and arrested. She unlocked the front door, and I asked her not to call the principal. As I placed my backpack on the bench in the foyer and took my shoes off, I asked her not to call the police. All the way to the back of the house and into the kitchen, I pleaded with her to drop the whole thing and not make a big deal out of it. But she continued to talk over me.

"I promise, Mom," I said and gave her tight a hug. "He's just a classmate who shares my disdain for high school parties."

She rolled her eyes but gave in with a sigh and a tight squeeze. "All right but promise me you'll be careful. If anything seems off or if he starts acting strange, you need to let me know immediately."

"I will, Mom," I promised and coughed repeatedly into my elbow.

"Hey, what's this?" she asked, narrowing her eyes at me.

I waved my hand dismissively and continued coughing, gasping for air.

She whipped out an inhaler from seemingly nowhere and held it to my mouth. "Breathe, Storm," she said soothingly.

I inhaled deeply, and she puffed the medicine into my mouth. The spray coated the back of my throat as I held my breath for as long as possible. My mother shook the inhaler again as she waited, and we repeated the process once more. Eventually, the tightness in my chest loosened and I could take a full breath without wheezing, air finding its way through my lungs again.

"Thanks, Mom," I said, my voice raspy.

She kissed my forehead over my long bangs. "Go and rinse."

I stepped away with the taste of the inhaler lingering in my mouth—slightly bitter and metallic—and went to my ensuite to wash my hands like a doctor preparing for surgery. Cupping the water in my palm, I rinsed my mouth. My hand shook. I was used to it—a side effect of the medicine. I grabbed a towel from the shelf and dried my face, staring at my reflection in the mirror.

These minor attacks were manageable, but how would I deal with a major attack once I was away at college? Mrs. Gladney, my counselor, had reiterated the basics: always carry an inhaler in your purse or backpack, ensure your room-mates, friends, and dorm leaders know what to do if you have symptoms, acquaint yourself with the campus health system, and know the location of the nearest hospital in case of an emergency.

I frowned. *What am I thinking? If my dream was real, I'll never make it to college—I'll be in heaven.*

"How are we doing?" Mom stood in the doorway, her hair pulled back in a tight ponytail. The light from the hallway cast a soft glow on her face, illuminating the worry lines on her forehead.

I wiped my mouth again. "That one just hit me out of nowhere, didn't it?" It was a poor attempt at making light of the moment.

She placed a comforting hand on my shoulder. "You know how unpredictable your asthma can be, Storm. That's why I worry so much."

"It's not *my* asthma. It's asthma. Can we say it like that? Just asthma?"

She nodded. "You're right. Wording is everything. But you have to be careful, kiddo."

"I know, Mom, and I appreciate you," I said with a smile.

"I was thinking about a swim . . ." she said. "Are you in?"

I wasn't surprised. All she talked about since I was a kid was how much swimming had strengthened my lungs and how if she had not encouraged me to swim, I would probably be dead.

"Right this minute?" I asked incredulously.

"No, silly, you know the rules. You have to rest at least 24 hours." She held her wrist up, setting a reminder alarm on her watch—the only person I knew who had alarms for almost everything. "Depends on how you feel tomorrow."

I nodded.

"And don't text that boy back."

"Mom . . . Are you seriously back on that?"

5

— · —

The next morning, I awoke before sunlight filtered through my curtains. I felt good—no wheezing or coughing.

The house was quiet, as though it was still asleep. I yawned and glanced around at my blue bedroom walls, which appeared gray under the dim glow of the fairy lights that made my room look like a bedroom on Pinterest. The bare wall was calling my name. I knew just what I wanted to add to my mural: flowers stretching from the back wall to the side walls in a sweeping arch.

I grabbed my phone to check the time and saw a text message. Although I expected it to come from Kendra, it was my mom, also up early. *How are you feeling today?*

I grinned and typed back: *How are you up already? I'm feeling great, ready to take on the day!*

That's good, honey. Remember to listen to your body and take it easy if you need to.

Me: *Go back to sleep, Mom.*

Neither one of us had to be up for a couple of hours. But, since I was wide awake, I turned on the overhead light, took out my respirator in case I did any painting, grabbed a pencil, and started sketching the flowers onto the next wall—following the sketch I'd done on paper.

Two hours later, I was already dressed and ready for the day when my mother came to check on me. "Oh, Storm," she said, examining the addition to the mural. "This is incredible. You've gotten so good."

A smile spread across my face as she approached the wall. "You like it? I've got skills, right?"

"Yes, but *that* we already know. The flowers are beautiful and those dandelion seeds blowing in the wind is a nice touch, even though a dandelion is technically a weed."

"Yeah, but it exists and just wants to be loved and find a place in this world like everything else."

She raised an eyebrow at me but couldn't hide her grin. "You're something else, Stormie."

I made a goofy face. "That's why you love me."

"That's part of it." She studied the wall again. "Nice . . ."

The school day wasn't much different from the day before. Teachers piling on school work with impossible deadlines as if they wanted us to move heaven and earth by the next day, seniors whispering about the party, classmates gossiping about the latest Netflix series ("Seriously, Storm, you have you seen it?"), Kendra obsessing over Pool like he's some kind of popstar, and Teresa desperately trying to convince me to join them at the swamp.

As promised, Mom and I went to the community center after school. It was just a short walk from our house, which made it convenient for us to go often. We were close to everything, actually. Beacon High was down the road, my old middle school was across the street from the high school, our church was behind our house, and the community center sat just around the corner.

We checked in with our center IDs and waved to the guy at the front desk who looked to be about twenty years old. He was more interested in doing bicep curls with the dumbbells he had taken from the gym, which I'm fairly certain were not supposed to be used in the office area, than watching us scan our cards.

The pool area had a strong smell of chlorine that, combined with the humid air, immediately stung my nostrils. It was a scent that instantly lifted my spirit, reminding me of countless summers spent at the outdoor community pool.

Through the open doorway, the water's glistening surface reflected the fluorescent lights above, creating a shimmering effect. Three lanes awaited us, marked by red ropes that trailed off into the deep end. On weekdays, the pool was mostly frequented by older adults and was quite peaceful—unlike the weekends, when the community center turned into a chaotic water park filled with shrieking children and their oblivious parents. But even amidst the chaos, there was one constant: Mrs. Tracey, the ever-smiling lifeguard who kept a watchful eye.

Mrs. Tracey, perched in her lifeguard chair and looking over at us, had worked at the community center since dinosaurs roamed the earth. She always welcomed us with a grin, wearing her signature neon yellow visor (although we were indoors), black bathing suit, and a whistle.

"Hey, Rebecca! Hey there, Storm! How's it goin'?" she shouted over the splashing water, greeting us like old friends.

"I'm good," I replied with a smile.

"That's great to hear! You know the drill," she said, gesturing toward the pool. "You're welcome to use lane one as usual,"

Lane three was the speed lane, lane two was the intermediate lane, and lane one was designated for slower swimmers. Lane one was best for the "sick girl."

In the ladies' locker room, I scrambled out of my clothes, fumbling with the swimsuit straps of my turquoise one-piece suit, before finally rushing out to the pool. To my delight, lane one was still unoccupied. *Score!*

A woman stood at the edge of the middle lane, wearing a flowery bathing cap. She gave me a nod before diving in with all the grace of a bulldozer.

I eased into lane one, letting my body adjust to the cool water. After slipping on my goggles, I took a deep breath and dove under. The water enveloped me, and I realized just how much I needed this. I swam back and forth, focusing on my breathing and form as I moved through the pool, my breaststroke steady and controlled. For a moment, I imagined myself competing at the Olympics—or at least the neighborhood swim meet.

My mom joined me after a few minutes, and we swam together for a while before she ditched me for the faster intermediate lane. Really, she was hovering, making sure I was okay.

Swimming was always therapeutic for me—not just because of its physical benefits, but because it gave me time to clear my mind and let go of any worries or stresses. I didn't care about swamp parties, whether the world was going to end, or who the boy was that texted me. There was no school drama or looming deadlines. Just me and the water gliding in sync. I even made up a rap in my head as I swam: *Freestyle flow, mind on hold, stress dissolves, story untold. Each stroke a verse, water my muse, worries dispersed, nothin' to lose.*

Wow, I'm really corny.

I reached the end of the lane and paused for a moment, resting my hands on the tiled wall, and watching my mother. Her strokes were effortless. She really should have swum in the speed lane, but she stayed in the intermediate lane to be close to me, though she would never admit it.

With a quick adjustment of my goggles, I dove back in for another lap.

Eventually, Mom signaled for us to leave. We emerged from the glistening water, droplets cascading from our bodies like liquid diamonds, and shuffled our way back to the locker room.

"I totally needed that," I chattered, reaching for a towel.

"Me too. Oh, I almost forgot!" She pulled out a beanie from her bag. "I brought you this because we have to walk home with wet hair. Let's hurry up."

"Why don't we ever shower here like everyone else?" I asked.

She scrunched up her face and wrinkled her nose. "Ew, have you smelled those communal showers?"

I shook my head. "Never mind."

Two hours later, after I was almost done drying my hair, Mom barged into my bathroom. "Murr cow!" she exclaimed.

I switched off the blow dryer. "What did you say?"

"Med count!" she repeated, with hands on her hips.

"Oh." I laughed about what I thought I heard. "Mom, it's done already."

She raised a brow. "Are you sure?"

"My inhalers are full, and I have one in my backpack, one in my purse, and one in my bedroom. *You* also have one downstairs in the kitchen drawer, one in your bedroom, and one in *your* purse. Don't worry, Mom. I'm stocked up for life."

"And your epinephrine auto-injector?"

The doorbell interrupted our conversation, and I was glad for it. "Expecting someone?"

"It's probably just a package," she said and hurried away.

"What did you order now, woman?" I asked jokingly. Like most moms, she ordered most of what we needed from Zigli-Cart rather than doing weekly grocery store runs.

A few seconds later, Kendra's cheerful voice belted my favorite words: "I've got dinner! J's Empanadas in the hizzy!"

I pushed a headband in place over the front of my hair and stared into my eyes in the mirror. The girl looking back at me looked unsure. I inhaled deeply and exhaled, feeling a slight pang in my chest. *You're okay, Storm*, I told myself and went down to the living room and embraced Kendra. "You're so silly."

She held a large paper bag with grease marks staining the bottom. "Oh, so I get love when I bring food, huh?"

"Did your dad make mine?" I grabbed for the bag, but Kendra pulled it out of my reach.

She gagged. "You mean the potato spinach ones? Unfortunately. It's a horrible thing to do to an empanada."

I finally managed to snatch the bag from her and cradled it lovingly against my chest. "But they're so good!"

Mom laughed. "Take it to the kitchen, ladies. And Kendra, thank your father for me. I don't know what we would do without our weekly empanadas. Tell him to not ever think about selling that food truck."

"I don't think he plans to. He's going to pick me up after some food truck party thingy downtown or whatever they call it. And since I didn't have to fill in for one of his staff tonight—you know, the one who hangs out the window taking the orders? Yeah, she's back—anyway I asked him to drop me off so I could bring you the Osso Bucco braised beef and the chicken, and there's some of my dad's mango salsa in there too. Oh, and yucca fries."

My mom's face lit up as she dug into the bag. "Seriously, Kendra, are you trying to make me fat? Because I'm eating all of this."

We settled around the kitchen table with paper plates over ceramic chargers. Sauce from the empanada dripped from the corner of my mouth onto my plate, as I took a bite. Kendra's father was truly an exceptional cook. I closed my eyes and savored the spices as I let out a moan of delight. "O-M-G. This stuff is like crack," I declared, greedily licking oil from my fingers.

"Storm, it's not that serious," said Kendra.

"Yes, it is. It's a spicy bite of heaven. You're just used to eating his cooking every day. Mom, tell her."

"I can't." She grinned sheepishly. "I can neither confirm nor deny that I may have inhaled the mango salsa straight from the container."

Kendra nearly toppled out of her chair from laughing when she realized my mother wasn't joking.

Between the empanadas and my mother's sweet potato brownies—which Kendra had no idea were actually made from sweet potatoes—by the time Kendra and I went up to my bedroom, we were stuffed.

Kendra flopped onto my bed and let out a dramatic sigh. "Why do you have the most comfiest bed in the world?"

I rolled my eyes. "Do I come over to your house and lay on your bed?"

"Yes, you do."

"Oh, well, carry on."

Kendra sat up suddenly. "Okay, not to be nosy or anything, but when I walked in, your mom questioned me about having one of your inhalers. Which I do, but is everything okay? Her eyes were a little red."

"I had an attack when I got home, but that was yesterday. What you saw was probably from swimming."

"Aww man, that sucks. But the attacks are still happening less often now, right?"

"Yeah."

She studied the sketch on my wall and pointed. "You've added to it. That's fire. So what do you think triggered this one? Too much homework? Not enough coffee? No boyfriend? Lack of fun, because you stay at home painting murals instead of going to senior parties?"

"Ken, you have the subtlety of a brick."

"Subtlety is not my strong suit. Sorry, not sorry."

"To answer your question, I don't know what brought it on. Can we please talk about something else? Like why you are here on a random Wednesday when your empanada deliveries are always on Thursdays?"

"Haha, busted. I couldn't resist being here for Teresa's call. I know, I know. Don't say it. I'm hopeless."

"I would've told you everything tomorrow."

"I didn't want to wait until tomorrow."

I shook my head. "Who knows how long they will be out there sneaking around in the dark doing who knows what. It's kind of gross when you think about it."

Kendra clutched my pillow to her chest with a mischievous grin. "I'm just curious, you know? Do a video call so I can see what they're up to."

"Curious or nosy?" I teased.

"Aren't they the same thing? Hey, this is not about me. It's all about Teresa right now. I'm looking out for her safety," she replied with a wink.

"All right, let's do it." I lay on my stomach at the foot of my bed, and Kendra lay beside me. We were shoulder-to-shoulder and head-to-head, my straight blonde hair pressed against her long braids, staring at my phone as it rang.

"Why isn't she answering?" Kendra wondered aloud.

I shrugged and set my phone down. "Maybe because she's in a swamp fighting off alligators?"

"Or she forgot her phone," Kendra replied.

"I doubt that. No, she probably has terrible cell reception out there."

Kendra rolled onto her back, flailing her arms and legs. "Or maybe because she's having the time of her life out there. She's having too much fun to pick up, I just know it."

I felt a bump on my chin and wandered into the bathroom to inspect it, shouting to Kendra, "Don't be jealous of them.

We're better than that. Plus, look at the night we're having here. Their swamp shenanigans can't top this."

She didn't respond.

"Oh, now you're giving me the silent treatment?"

When I returned to the room, I found Kendra hunched over my desk with my notebook open, looking completely baffled.

"What the heck is this?"

6

M y jaw clenched as I quelled the tempest building within me. "Give me that!" I snapped.

Kendra flinched back in surprise at my tone and dropped my notebook on the desk. "Oh, you're mad? Well, prepare to blow a gasket because I want to know what this means. The end of the world?"

"Since when do you go through my stuff?" I asked as I snatched the book from the desk.

"Duh, since forever. We're as close as twins. We have no secrets."

Kendra looked hurt, and I felt bad for barking at her, but there was no way I was going to tell her the truth and sound like a complete idiot for believing in a dream.

"Well?" Kendra demanded, plopping back down on the end of my bed like a stubborn toddler waiting for an answer.

I sat in the wicker chair that hung from the ceiling in the corner of my room. It was the only thing I begged my mother for when I was thirteen—the perfect spot to sit and read.

Now, it mostly just collected dust, but at least it was a pretty backdrop in photos.

Kendra stared at me and wouldn't look away. I don't think she even blinked.

"Okay. So . . . I'm working on this story and the part you read is where I got stuck. You know, writer's block? Mrs. Caplan talked about it last week when that author gave a presentation and discussed her writing process. I know she came to your class too."

Kendra's face softened. "Is that all? Why didn't you just say so?" She reached for the notebook. "Give it here."

I hesitated before handing it over.

"How did you come up with this story?" Kendra asked, flipping through the pages.

"I, uh, had a very bizarre dream," I admitted, feeling slightly embarrassed.

"Well, it sounds terrifying. You've written the events that are supposed to happen. But . . ." She looked up at the ceiling. "What if they don't? No, that's not what I mean. What if they had alternate outcomes that could lead to a different type of an apocalypse—not the typical quote, unquote, apocalypse we've read about, you know? That's some twisted plot twist, right?"

I grinned at her. "You're right."

"Look at me, a junior helping out a senior with her writing. I don't know why you didn't ask me in the first place." She grabbed a pen. "I'll write that here for you."

I snatched the pen from her. "No, let me do it. I want it all in my handwriting."

"Okay, okay, Miss Bossy. Are we good now?"

"When were we not?" I asked with a smirk.

"What time is it?"

"Too early for Teresa to be home."

Kendra fell back on my bed. "Man, they need to hurry this up."

"Can I ask you a question?"

"Yepper."

"Real talk . . . What if you knew the date the world would end? Like, it was coming up soon. What would you do differently?"

Kendra sat up and stared at my closet door. "For real?"

"Yeah, for real. What would you do?"

"And there's nothing I can do about it, right?"

"Right."

Kendra's eyes widened. "Wait, like a zombie apocalypse or asteroid collision?"

"Really, Kendra?"

"Yeah, there's a difference."

"Okay. Umm . . . let's go with the asteroid collision."

"I'd probably finally ask that cute barista out on a date."

I snorted. "Stop playing, he's like twenty-two."

"And maybe skydive naked. Oh! And try every flavor of Ben & Jerry's in one sitting." She gestured excitedly. "Oh, oh, oh! We should make a bucket list of all the craziest things to do before the end!"

"Yeah, all righty. Can you be serious for a minute?"

Kendra's smile faded. "I don't know, Storm. Love on my family, I guess. Umm . . . Pray for forgiveness for the things I've done wrong."

"Would you tell people?"

"Who would believe me? That's tough. Oh, I know, I'd plant one on Pool, for only a second—okay, maybe five—and show him what he missed out on."

I grabbed my pillow and playfully whacked her on the back of her head.

"Well, at least I'd go to heaven knowing if his lips were soft or not."

I shook my head. "Therapy, that's what you need. You've got some real issues going on in that head."

"Right back at you, sis. You're the only girl in school who isn't boy-crazy. Why is that?"

"Maybe because I'm just trying to live and breathe on a daily basis."

"As is the world."

"You know what I mean, Ken. It'll take a special boy to deal with all of that."

"He's out there, Storm. You'll get yourself a kiss before the world ends." She laughed and retaliated with a pillow smack.

"Oh, wait." I pulled out my phone. "He may be closer than you think. You've gotta see these texts I received after school." I showed Kendra the screen, watching her jaw drop.

Kendra gasped. "You've been keeping this from me?"

"Only since yesterday." I held a hand up. "In my defense, I had an attack yesterday. I didn't get a chance to mention it until now."

She squealed with excitement and bounced on my bed as if it were a trampoline. "Who do you think it is?"

"I haven't a clue. Nor do I know how he got my number."

Kendra stood and turned away from me so that all that I saw were braids.

"Kendra?"

I circled her, and as I did, she kept turning so I couldn't see her face.

"You know who he is, don't you?"

"Isn't the sharing of personal information illegal at school? Shame on them."

"Kendra," I said slowly. "The school doesn't have my cell phone number. Who is he?"

"All I'm going to say is make sure you wear something cute tomorrow."

"Kendra!"

She bolted out of the bedroom, and I charged after her, down the stairs and out the front door. Kendra stopped on the lawn and lifted her hands. "Whoa, I didn't really expect you to chase me," she said, looking concerned. "Are you okay?"

"I'm fine," I replied and held up my inhaler, just as my mother came running up behind me. "What's happening out here?"

"Nothing. Just Kendra Kendraing."

"Did you just make me a verb?"

Kendra barreled toward me while I hid behind my mother, backing her up into the house. "Mom, save me!" I cried. She laughed as we playfully dodged around her.

"All right girls, that's enough. Settle down now," my mom commanded with a smile.

Kendra flung herself on the sofa. "Dang, Storm, you didn't have an attack from all of that?"

"I'm pretty impressed, myself. Mom . . ."

"Hmmm?"

"Guess what?"

"Chicken butt?"

Kendra and I burst into laughter even though it had to be the corniest joke she had ever made.

"No, Mom. Kendra gave that boy my number."

Kendra shot me a look, and I took off up the stairs with her close behind.

"Hey! Cool it, you two," my mom yelled.

As soon as we got to my room, we collapsed onto my bed.

"Whew, my thighs burn. I seriously need to do stairs more often," said Kendra.

After that, we laughed, took selfies, and played games on our phones until Mr. J arrived to pick up Kendra. He was a gentleman and never honked or texted Kendra to come out. He always came to the door or inside and chatted with us for a while before taking her home.

"Sup, Mr. J?" I exclaimed as I swung open the door.

He threw up a hand. "Did I nail it? Tell me I nailed it!"

I gave him a fist bump. "Killed it. Like always, the empanadas were amazing. Mom! Kendra's dad is here!"

She emerged from the kitchen. "Oh, *there's* the reason I've put on ten pounds. Thank you for your assistance with that, Julius.

"No worries, I've got you," he replied, then laughed until he turned red.

"What's so funny?" my mom asked.

He pointed at her feet. "Those Grinch slippers."

"Hey, I like these. They're comfy."

"Storm," Kendra whispered and poked me in the side. "I think your mom has a thing for Afro-Latinos. She's totally vibing with my dad. Watch the body language. She's leaning into him. She likes his dreads, doesn't she?" she joked and nudged me. "I bet you're mixed. You could be mixed. Like Mariah Carey. I bet you are."

"Or maybe they're just lifelong friends since, you know, he was the one who delivered me and all."

"Or that," she said with a grin.

"Mr. J, could you please take her home?" I asked as I pushed Kendra to the door.

"Absolutely, let's go, troublemaker," he said, gently grabbing her shoulders and guiding her outside to the truck. "Did you remember to do your homework?"

"Oops, I forgot," Kendra replied.

"Kendra . . ." Mr. J scolded, muttering something in Spanish.

"It's your fault. You handed me the empanadas, so I forgot my backpack."

"My fault?" he asked.

Kendra stepped into the truck and pulled the door shut. As the engine started, she suddenly rolled down the window and stuck her head out. "Storm! Text me as soon as you hear from Teresa, okay?"

"Okay!" I yelled back.

Her eyes locked on mine for a moment, as though she was making sure I understood before disappearing back into the truck.

I waved and shut the door.

My mom shook her head. "She's quite a whirlwind, isn't she?"

"She sure is." The way I saw it, it made sense that we were friends; I had a storm constantly brewing inside of me, while she was like a whirlwind—always energetic and unpredictable.

7

After an evening with Kendra, I didn't wake as my usual energized self, ready to take on the world. And working on my mural was the last thing on my mind. My alarm blared, and I reached over and hit the snooze button. Five minutes later, it went off again, and I hit snooze.

The cycle repeated nine more times until I finally dragged myself out of bed, groggy and ignoring my mom yelling, "Storm, get up! It's 6:47!"

The whole end-of-the-world conversation with Kendra still lingered at the back of my mind, though I now dismissed the details as just being another dream.

Unlike my memories, my dreams gradually faded like they never happened—kind of like after Hurricane Ithaca swept through Florida and wreaked havoc on us on its way to the Atlantic.

For days, the community worked to clean up the debris left behind, mainly branches and fallen oak trees. My mom was livid because she had to hire a repairman to fix our roof (thanks a lot, Ithaca), but so did everyone else in town. Eventually, life returned to normal. The swamp receded from Tommy Morrison's backyard, leaving behind a five-foot gator he called Willie and took pictures of—from his back porch—daily. Gas trucks refilled stations, power was restored, and restaurants reopened.

Now it's like it never happened. Except for the massive tree stump in our backyard that we turned into a makeshift seat for our firepit. Thanks again, Ithaca.

I dressed, snapped a quick selfie, and texted it to Kendra: *Today's look. Are we twinning?*

Kendra responded quickly: *R U kidding? Is that UR mom's? Get cuter!*

I groaned, changed into another outfit, and sent another picture: *What about now?*

Kendra: *Meh, I'm not feeling it.*

Fed up, I stripped down to my bra and panties and took another photo: *What about this?!*

Kendra: *PERFECT! Now we're twinning for real!*

Twinning? Kendra wasn't dressed either? She had a whole skincare regimen before she got dressed, plus a makeup routine after that. Her skill was in mastering the "no-makeup look" so her father wouldn't have a conniption.

Just as I was about to respond to her text, my mother barged in, seeing me giggling and the phone in my hand. "Storm! Are you sending nude pictures to that boy?"

The shock on her face only made me laugh harder. "No, and I'm not naked. Here, look. I'm messing with Kendra."

She read the texts. "Oh, then tell her to delete that one."

"Mom, did you really think I would do something like that?"

"Of course not. You're a good girl," she replied as she closed my bedroom door.

I shook my head, then inspected myself in the mirror and winced at the new bruise on my leg. Thanks a lot, corticosteroids.

I texted Kendra: *My mom said delete that pic.*

Kendra: *Done.*

I threw on some baggy cargo pants and an oversized sweatshirt that I thought, when I pulled my hair back, made me look a lot like my favorite singer, M. R. Ward. I sent Kendra another selfie, fully expecting her to appreciate my look.

Kendra: *Are you serious right now?*

Me: *As an asthma attack. Where's yours?*

Kendra replied with a photo of jeans and a sweatshirt sprawled on her bed instead of on her body.

I texted back: *Works for me.*

That was us most mornings because we shopped together and often showed up dressed exactly alike, like fashion soulmates or something. People thought we planned it, but we were just in sync that way.

"Cup of tea, my dear?" my mom asked with a dramatic British accent as I set my backpack in a chair at the kitchen table.

The smell of chamomile immediately put me at ease. I nodded and leaned against the island. "Thanks, Mom," I said, wrapping my hands around the warm mug. The steam rose gently, caressing my face. It was a comforting routine, one that I cherished every morning and would miss once I went off to college.

As I sipped, I glanced at the clock, feeling surprisingly giddy with anticipation. Why was I so excited about meeting this boy? For all I knew he could look like Quasimodo.

I glanced at my phone, noticing a new message from Kendra: *Hey, are you ready to R&B the day?*

Me: *R&B it?*

Kendra: *I didn't want to say rock the day. I changed it to R&B.*

A smile tugged at the corners of my lips as I typed back: *Oh, LOL. As ready as I'll ever be. Making memories before the end of the world.*

Kendra: *Oh yeah. Ha! Your story. Time's a-ticking! Plot twist: we're actually living in a zombie apocalypse.*

Me: *OMG don't even joke about that.*

Kendra: *I'm outside. Are you driving me or what?*

"T hanks for the ride!" Kendra blew a kiss at my mother as she pulled off.

"Please stop doing that. It's so weird."

"You know she's practically my stepmom."

I rolled my eyes at her.

"But what's really weird is getting rides to school when you live right down the street," she quipped.

I shrugged. "It's what she likes to do. Think about it. It's such a short ride that there's not enough time to bring up big things—grades, graduation, college—so we can just talk about silly stuff. I think it helps her pretend I'm not leaving soon."

Kendra twisted open a tube of lip gloss and dabbed it onto her lower lip. "I'm glad I still have a year before all that madness." she responded, pressed her lips together, puckered, and made a kissy face at herself in her pocket mirror.

I leaned in, inspecting her lip gloss choice. "Ooh, sparkly. Who are you trying to impress today?"

"No one. But, come to think of it, here! Put some on."

"I already have some," I replied, swatting hers away.

We walked across the grid. Tires squealed, and a Land Rover pulled in front of us and parked. Pool stepped out with a confident grin and winked in our direction. The car beeped as he locked it, and he sauntered off, slow and deliberate, knowing all the girls in the vicinity eyed him.

"Wow," was all Kendra said, while I scanned the kids pouring out of the school buses in the next lot. Teresa's orange jacket usually made it easy to spot her; if you knew her well enough, you knew orange was her favorite color. It was rare to see anyone else wearing such a bright shade.

"Where is she?" I wondered aloud and took out my phone and called her. She didn't pick up.

Kendra silently watched until I placed my phone back in my pocket. "Is she ghosting us?"

Car horns honked as they maneuvered around us to the parking spaces. I shook my head and pulled her over to the grass. "I don't know."

Kendra stood on her toes, scanning the parking lot as more cars pulled in. Her eyes darted from one to the next, looking for Teresa's car. "She wasn't on the school bus, and she didn't drive. Maybe she got a ride today and is already here. Let's find her before first period."

"We better hurry then. Our classes are on opposite sides of the building."

I led the way, joining the flow of students moving at varying paces, navigating toward the school's entrance. Some were focused on their textbooks, while others moved slowly, deep in conversation or scrolling on their phones. Every now and then, a loud shriek of recognition echoed through the air as friends reunited, as if they hadn't seen each other the day before.

The entrance grew congested as acquaintances exchanged nods, hugs, headlocks, or fist bumps. Kendra and I weaved through the crowd and down past the lockers to the media center.

"Why did we come this way? I would think she'd be in the courtyard, hanging out with Pool and his friends."

"True, but I'm not thinking as positively as you are. If something went wrong last night, Teresa wouldn't be there."

"Assuming something actually went wrong," said Kendra.

The media center door slid closed behind us, sealing off the hallway chatter.

"She's been coming here in the mornings to work on the presentation for her senior project. She said a few people are helping her with it, but I don't know the details," I told Kendra and checked the clock on the wall. "We've got five minutes. Let's split up. Go that way."

Kendra gave a quick nod before zipping off toward the seating area. The media center had a sea vibe with various shades of blue and green everywhere. Its color scheme was probably supposed to relax us, but I found it depressing. It reminded me of when I was a kid and had broken or lost most of my crayons—these blues and greens were always the last colors available in the crayon box when I really wanted a red.

I walked around a girl lying on her stomach reading on a small green sofa. Across from her, a boy sat in a blue chair with his feet propped up on a sea moss green ottoman, his head back and mouth open, snoring. Kendra ran to another set of sofas, and I went over to the computer stations, only to be met with curious glances from each student, as if I was invading their privacy.

Next, I rushed up and down the book aisles and came out just as Kendra emerged from the other side. "No luck. She's not here. I'm going to class."

"See you at lunch," Kendra said and hurried away. Her long braids disappeared down the hallway, the faded denim jacket she wore over her sweatshirt blending in with the flow of students.

On my way to class, I passed by the courtyard where Pool hung out, unconcerned about the late bell, as if he were above the laws of Beacon High. Lots of laughter and obnoxious conversations floated through the open doors. I glanced at the picnic tables and benches, but there wasn't a spot of orange out there. No Teresa.

Oh well, I tried. I shrugged it off, telling myself she might be out sick or somewhere else in the building.

Pool frantically gestured for me to join them, but I shook my head and pointed down the hall. He shrugged and mimicked my gestures, laughed at himself, and then nodded and gave me a thumbs up.

The bell rang just as I entered class and took my seat.

"The Storm is here!" said Mario, earning a few laughs from around the room. "Where are the rest of the X-Men?" He continued with his corny jokes, as if I hadn't heard the same ones a thousand times already.

I rolled my eyes and ignored the giggles that followed. Especially those coming from Pool's current girlfriend, Tiffany Lancaster.

"They're with your mama," retorted a boy on the other side of the room, causing a chorus of "Oohs" to erupt.

I looked over my shoulder at him. He fist bumped the air and I grinned and fist bumped back. I turned to face the front of the room again, feeling my face reddening. *Was it him who sent the texts? Todd?*

Mrs. Collins took attendance, then droned on about chemical reactions. I discreetly glanced over at Todd, trying to decipher any clues from his expression. He was surprisingly attentive, eagerly taking notes and even raising his hand to answer questions.

At the end of class, with the sound of the bell echoing in my ears, I packed up my things and mentally prepared myself to do something completely out of character. *It's now or never*, I thought as I mustered up the courage to approach Todd. I mean, what did I have to lose? It wasn't like he had ever taken up for me before. He barely even knew I existed—except for that time in gym class when I hit him in the face with a volleyball. That was the best serve of my life, but it never made it over the net and hit him in the face. Why was he facing me anyway?

Todd was busy talking to his friends when he noticed me approaching. Surprise flickered across his face before it settled into a smile. He had a million freckles, and I thought they added to his looks.

"Hey," I said, trying to sound casual. "Thanks for your help earlier, I mean for defending me."

Todd cheeks reddened. "No problem. Had to show some support for 'The Storm,' you know?"

I nodded, playing along. "Yeah, it's nice to have some loyal fans."

"Yo, I'll catch you outside," his friend said, pointing behind him at the door.

I looked back just in time to see his other friends giving him several thumbs up. One of them passionately kissed his notebook.

"Ignore those weirdos. They have no home training."

"Clearly. Hey, not to be random or anything, but did you send me a text?"

His brows furrowed. "You received a text from me?"

Heat rose from my sweatshirt collar. "Well, I—I don't know who sent it."

Todd slung a strap of his backpack over his shoulder. "Ooh . . . a secret admirer. There are a lot of guys who want that spot. Have you tried calling the number the text came from?"

I mentally face-palmed. *Why didn't I think of that?* I knew why. The mystery of it all was so intriguing, like my favorite movie, *To All the Boys I've Loved Before.*

Wait, what guys wanted that spot?

My eyes went from the floor to the desk to the left of us. "No, I haven't done that yet."

"Well, when you do, tell him I said he's a lucky guy."

Wait, what?

Todd turned to leave, and I remembered seeing him with Pool.

"Hey, wait. Todd, you know Teresa, right? The one with the . . ." I gestured toward my chest. "Have you seen her?"

Todd's eyes widened briefly. "Oh yeah, Teresa. She was hanging out with Pool last night. Man, she was wasted."

"Wasted? Teresa doesn't drink. Are you sure you saw her?"

"Umm hmm," he replied as if it was nothing of concern. "Pool drove her home."

Mystery solved. "Uh, okay. Thanks."

The news left me with a mix of relief and frustration. I was worried about a girl I wasn't exactly tight with anymore, when none of this was any of my business. The least she could do was answer my calls or texts.

At least she made it home. Her drinking would explain why she wasn't at school. She probably had a hangover, and I knew all about those.

By lunchtime my stomach grumbled as if I hadn't eaten in a week, so I hurried to the cafeteria. Before I could get inside, the smell of mystery meat and nacho cheese wafted through the air. Pool and his buddies were already seated at their usual table. My eyes darted around the crowd, bouncing from face to face, searching for any sign of Kendra or anyone else I would want to sit with.

"Boo!"

I jumped and swung a hand at Kendra. "Stop doing that."

Kendra and I scrambled to grab our lunches from the crowded line. Then she nudged me toward a table by the windows—where she would have a good view of Pool.

As usual, Pool sat on top of the table with his friends huddled around him, engaging in a lively conversation as we passed by. Tiffany Lancaster spotted me and shot an annoyed glance in my direction before whispering something to Pool. The group fell silent as they all turned their attention toward me.

"Hey, Storm," Pool called out, a smug grin playing on his lips. "Looking for someone?"

9

The way I heard it from the neighbors who gathered on our front lawn at dusk, gossiping, the cost of living was getting so high in larger cities that people were flocking to small towns like Spencer, and the community was mad about it. But what happens when a city grows? It gets cool stores that the rest of the world has, like Costco. We even have a Starbucks, Red Lobster, and Taco Bell now.

But one thing that hasn't changed? The gossip mill at Beacon High. Seriously, if someone farts in the hallway, they might as well have broadcasted it on the morning announcements because everyone knows about it by lunch. So I wasn't surprised Pool had found out I was looking for Teresa.

I shrugged and sat with my tray. A seat farther away would've been ideal, but at the height of cafeteria chaos, there weren't any tables with enough room for both me and Kendra to squeeze into.

Kendra sat beside me and stared Tiffany—a.k.a. "queen bee" of the school—down, shooting daggers with her eyeballs, until Tiffany finally backed off and turned away. "Sheesh, what's her problem?"

"You need to narrow that down. Do you mean at this particular moment or this hour, because she's always got a problem."

"Noted," Kendra replied with a laugh.

I peeled off the paper from my straw and glanced around us. "Oh, I found out something."

"About Teresa?" Kendra asked and stopped rubbing her fingers with her sanitary wipe.

I nodded and lowered my voice. "Whatever they did last night, they were drinking. I heard that Teresa got wasted—like, really trashed."

"Shut up, no way!"

"Yeah."

"Dang, you were right. Don't go anywhere with them."

"Hadn't planned to."

"Well . . . maybe just Pool," Kendra replied, with a dreamy gaze in his direction.

"Stop being so obvious. You look thirsty. Oh! Hey, I know who the guy is, the one who texted me."

"You do?"

"Yeah, it's Todd."

"Who's that?" she asked.

I pointed across the cafeteria.

"Where?"

"Behind the girl with the cupcake frosting on her lips."

"Oh. Nope, that's not him."

"Are you sure?"

"Positive. That guy is totally giving me *Maze Runner* vibes."

"Don't you mean someone from the movie? Who, Newt? How could he look like the entire cast?"

She smirked. "He looks like he could be in the movie—you know, running in the glade."

I let out a snort of laughter, realizing how ridiculously accurate she was. Like seriously, spot on. "Stop it, Ken. I think he's cute."

"I think you want it to be him, but it's not."

"I'm going to call the number he texted from."

"Don't, Storm. Just wait. Have some faith. You trust me, right?"

I squinted. "Mostly."

Kendra erupted into a fit of giggles. "Okay, I know I've had a few crazy stunts, but I promise you'll be glad you waited."

I chewed on my straw, pretending not to care as I glanced over at Todd. *We shall see.*

As we ate and listened to the noisy conversations around us, my eyes darted across the cafeteria, searching for a boy who might be discreetly watching me—maybe one I never noticed before. *What if he isn't a senior?* I dismissed the thought and finished my lunch. Boys were immature. I wanted no parts of an underclassman.

During my next class, while discussing the civil rights movement, my day took a turn for the worst.

"What did that sick girl just say?" came from Tiffany Lancaster.

"Another word from you and you can kiss your diploma goodbye," said Mr. Whittle. With a quick tug at the thigh of his slacks, he sat on the edge of his desk. "Go ahead, Storm."

"Black people definitely made huge strides on their own, but I think to amplify their message, they needed white people too. Well, not need—"

"Why would you say that?" asked Levi, the girl beside me.

"Power to the people!" a girl shouted and raised a fist in the air. Many of my classmates laughed, while the girl behind me continuously kicked my chair. The beat to a death march.

Tiffany Lancaster crumpled a piece of paper and flung it at the girl still holding up her fist. "You're not even Black, Daniela."

"No, I get what she's saying," said Todd, once again coming to my defense. "We all need each other."

"Shut up, Todd. Nobody asked you," said Tiffany Lancaster.

"Then stop trying to go all militant."

"That's exactly what I'm saying," I replied. "I think that for real change to happen, we must all play some part in bringing about that change."

From that reasoning, I got a, "Okay, that's true," "She's right," and a "Dr. Storm Luther King had a dream"—sparking a much larger debate, while other classmates looked at me like I had three heads. I regretted opening my big mouth. It didn't matter that my best friend was Afro-Puerto Rican, some of my classmates still acted like they thought I was racist.

"You need to learn more about my history," Cicely, another classmate, said as she passed me after class.

Great. There goes my good girl, Storm loves everyone, image. Now I'll be labeled as the ignorant, racist, idiotic "sick girl". Maybe I still needed to learn what to say—and what not to say—to avoid offending people of other races, which was never my intention in the first place. *There goes my A+ in cultural sensitivity.*

While mentally beating myself up, I caught a glimpse of Todd's lanky figure ahead of me in the hallway and, for a moment, all my worries vanished. *It's him, I know it. Kendra tried to throw me off. She's so sneaky.*

I trailed behind Todd. He was completely clueless, lost in his own little world of comic books and drum machines—I remembered seeing him with that stuff before. Meanwhile, I counted down the seconds until he finally looked over his shoulder and noticed me. "Hurry up, Todd, before the world ends!" I whispered to myself with a laugh. The phrase had become my refrain whenever I awaited something, as though I believed the apocalypse dream was going to come true. But he didn't look back even once before turning down another corridor, away from the class I was headed to.

Oh, come on!

What I had played out in my mind was him stopping and saying, "Hey, Storm. I see you back there. Those were my texts. I was too shy to admit it was me. Want to go to prom with me?"

Why are boys so complicated? Ugh, just admit it, and we can move on.

I moped around, wallowing in my Todd-induced misery for the rest of the afternoon. After calculus, I stopped at my locker and grabbed my jacket off the hook inside. Just as I closed the door, Todd approached.

My heart skipped a beat. *It's him. He was waiting until after school to talk to me. I knew it. Here he comes.* Todd waved, and I held my breath. *What should I do? Lean against my locker? I don't know how to pose. Where is Kendra when I need her?*

But typical Todd walked right past me without even a second glance. I looked back, watching him disappear through the crowd.

"Yo, Storm!"

I whipped around, coming face to face with the boy that I had almost bumped into a few days before. *What's her name's older brother . . . What is her name? Mandy? Joyce? No, no, it's something cooler. Jade or Josie or . . . Juliana! That's it.*

"Hey, I'm Raine."

"Yes, I know who you are."

"Right, because you know Jill and—ah, okay. Listen, I have a proposition for you."

Oh, it's Jilliana, not Juliana. I closed my locker and folded my arms across my chest. Raine was biracial and had the curliest, wildest hair that was oddly so attractive. He also had a strong presence. You never wanted to get into an argument with him because he possessed a remarkable ability to skillfully wield words as sharp as swords, cutting people down and leaving them speechless. The girls stalked him as much as they did Pool.

"I have this podcast and Andrea is sick—a bad case of the flu. She's my cohost. We need that female perspective, you know? So I thought you might want to fill in for her. Plus, I heard about your opinions in class today, and that's exactly what I'm looking for."

I rolled my eyes. That had to be a new record for how fast news spread through Beacon High. "A podcast? Really? I don't know anything about podcasts."

"But you've listened, right?"

"Occasionally. But why me? You don't even know me."

"Oh, I think I do. Let's see," he said as he squinted and tapped his pointer finger on his lips. "You're interesting, actually more so than most of these wipeouts."

"Wipeouts?"

"Yeah, they crash under the waves of knowledge. Everything goes right over their heads, plunging them into the depths of the sea."

That was deep. Why does he have such effortless coolness?

"Well, I don't totally disagree with that."

"I didn't think you would. May I continue?"

"If you must."

Raine squinted at me again and then glanced at the ceiling as he spun a full 360 on his heels. "You're involved in everything, and I mean everything: you play the viola in the school orchestra, you're on the student council, you're on the chess and debate teams, and I bet the walls of your bedroom are some shade of blue and covered in all of your crafts and art projects and maybe even a mural because you're in the art club." He held up his pointer finger. "Now, what people don't know, and what you may not even admit to yourself, is that you do all these things, except sports, because you believe it's a way of truly living life to its fullest—because you think your life is going to be cut short because of your asthma." He met my gaze, his eyes gleaming with a mix of confidence and satisfaction. His brows arched slightly, daring me to challenge his insight. Then he crossed his arms like he had just solved a puzzle no one else could. "How did I do?"

How did he do? Is he serious? Where is a security officer when I need one? I narrowed in on his hazel eyes. "How did you know all of that? You've been stalking me?"

"Please. I prefer the term 'observing'," he replied with a smirk. There wasn't a shy bone in this guy's body.

I took a step back, feeling exposed.

"Look, at least consider filling in for Andrea for this week's episode, just as a favor. After that, you can determine if you like it and want to do another." He grinned. "I'm harmless, I promise."

"I doubt that. After how you just *read* me, I don't sound that interesting. And you didn't answer my first question."

"Which was what?"

"Why me?"

"Oh, I thought that was obvious. Raine and Storm. Get it? It's kind of cool, right? We could get married, have a kid, and name him Tsunami." He glanced away. "Sorry, I don't know why I said that. So will you?"

I hesitated. "I don't know. My schedule—"

"We can work around it. You can even choose the topics. We will talk about whatever you want, okay? Do we have a deal? Storm, please don't make me do it . . ."

"Do what?"

"You're going to do it, aren't you?" he asked as he grimaced. "You're going to make me beg?"

I suppressed the urge to burst out laughing as Raine placed the palms of his hands together as though he were praying. He pouted and pleaded with those puppy dog eyes, and bent his knees, lowering just enough until he was looking up at me. I could barely see his pupils through his long dark lashes.

The hall cleared out fast, as it often did unless there were after-school activities like a game or event. Down the corridor, Kendra bounced excitedly, having witnessed our exchange. She waved and pointed at her phone before scurrying out the side door.

"Come on, it would look great on your college applications also."

"Already accepted. What else you got?" I was curious but I didn't tell him that.

"We could vent about the absurdity of high school parties in swamps?"

My eyes widened and focused on his face, like a camera lens zooming in for a close-up and holding the frame. "It was you . . ." I uttered slowly, suddenly really seeing him. "You sent the texts." *Not Todd?*

"Guilty," Raine said with a grin, revealing his dimple.

I don't know what he expected me to say next, but I think he confused my silence with needing to be convinced further.

"And that selfie of you in your unmentionables was stellar."

"What?" I sputtered. Raine's words hit me like a sledgehammer to the chest. My mind went blank with shock and disbelief. I couldn't process what was happening. The tears started as an uncontrollable flood, soaking my cheeks and staining my shirt.

Raine looked confused. "Wait. Why are you—"

I tried to speak through my sobs, but he pulled me into a tight embrace before I could finish. Sharp gasps came from me as I buried my face into his shoulder, trying to muffle the sound.

"I'm sorry. I didn't know you would react like this. It was a joke. Kendra didn't tell me you were so sensitive. She said you would think it was funny. She didn't show me anything. I promise."

I pulled away from him and dried my eyes. "Kendra told you that?"

"Yeah. Why would you cry about it? That's no way to handle a situation. I pegged you as being more logical than that."

"Why would I cry? Because I don't let people see me like that. I was almost naked!"

He raised an eyebrow, a mocking smirk playing on his lips. "But you *did* send her the picture, right? Why would you do something so stupid? You know that kind of stuff is forever. Sure, she deleted it, but you know it can always be recovered and come back to haunt you when you least expect it. You're smarter than that, Storm."

"Stop talking to me like you know me." I turned to walk away, before I embarrassed myself any further.

"All right, all right," he said quickly and grabbed my arms, turning me back to face him as he leaned into my face. "Say you'll join me, please?"

I nodded.

"Yes!" Raine exclaimed and spun while swinging his hands in the air. It seemed he had a tendency to spin, as if he were constantly caught on some invisible carousel. "This completes my vision. You have no idea how much this means."

"No," I added coldly. The nod was just me clearing my head. I wasn't agreeing to anything.

"Huh?" His brows knit together in confusion.

"You and Kendra have worked things out this far. Maybe she can help you find someone else's feelings to manipulate and hurt." I walked away. "Oh," I said and stopped. "There's a new girl who assists in the office—Sunny or Windy or something. Her name fits, right? Ask *her*."

"Storm . . ." Raine called after me.

"Lose my number! Jerk."

10

A gust of wind tousled my blonde-highlighted waves as I bolted out of a set of the school double doors. My body was so warm from getting emotional that I welcomed the March chill.

My mother stood outside her car door, watching me as I exited. She waved me forward, though I could feel Raine's gaze behind me calling me back. I knew he was there. He wouldn't chase me. He wasn't the type. But he would watch from a distance.

I hurried across the sidewalk.

"Stormie, if you're running late, just text me. We've talked about this before."

"Sorry," I said and sat in the front passenger seat. I looked out my window at the school, spotting Raine at the main doors with his hands in the pockets of his jacket. Our eyes met just for a moment. I was angry with Raine, but something else lingered from our exchange that I couldn't put into words. "Mom, can you just go?"

"Tough day?"

"Something like that."

"Ah, high school drama. So glad those days are long gone," she said and started the car.

"I envy you." I sighed, sinking into the seat as all the negative events of the day took center stage in my mind, one after another.

She studied me for a moment and pulled the car away from the curb. We drove in silence and were cruising by a gas station when I realized we hadn't pulled into our driveway. I sat up. "Uh, Mom? Did you forget how to get to our house?"

She glanced over and gently ran a curled finger down my cheek. "Well, by the look on your face, and after the day I've had, I'm taking a little detour. I'd say we can both use a strong drink."

"You've got that right." I let out a dramatic sigh, slumping back in my seat.

"What happened?"

My mother never let things go, so I had to tell her something, and I didn't want to talk about Raine. "Mom, am I like, accidentally racist?"

She held back a laugh. "That's absurd. Why would you think that?" She shook her head. "That's not even possible. You were raised in a multicultural community."

"I know. And we went to D.C. to the Black History Museum and everything, but people act like . . . I don't know . . . I don't want to be racist."

"You're not."

"Well, some of the kids at school sure seem to think so."

"Why? Because you're white?"

"No, because of something I said. Mom, don't you think Black and white people had to work together for civil rights? My classmates acted like that was the craziest thing they ever heard. I mean, there were no Black people in Congress. How do they think things changed? We had to work together. Teamwork makes the dream work. And, hello, I know what I'm talking about because I'm on the friggen debate team, for goodness' sake."

"You make a good point. But you're also incorrect."

I sat up. "I am?"

"The civil rights movement spanned from when?"

"Ummm . . . 1954 to1968."

"Shirley Chisholm was the first Black female elected to Congress in 1968, but there were males before her. Even in class discussions, you should abide by the rules you follow for the debate team."

"Mom . . ." I groaned and shifted in my seat.

"No, seriously, Storm. Listen. You must be able to provide evidence or reasons to support your statement. And facts presented in a debate must be accurate."

"I know," I muttered. My head dropped. I thought talking about it would make me feel better. Now I felt worse. "I didn't mention the Congress thing in class, though."

"Oh, well, that's different. And don't say friggen."

"I got it from you! You say friggen all the time."

"I'm an adult and allowed to break the rules." She rubbed my arm. "You're not racist, Stormie. My father was. You're not. I wouldn't have it."

I stared straight ahead at the traffic light, unblinking. My mother slipped up, and by the new tension in the air and the awkward silence that followed, she realized it. *She mentioned something about my grandfather. She never mentions anyone. He was racist?* I played it off, acting like she didn't say anything the slightest bit unusual.

"It's so crowded this afternoon." I pointed. "There's a parking space over there."

"Oh, good. I see it."

I grabbed the handle of my door and held on for dear life as my mom whipped Betty into the tight space at Phelps Plaza, with the speed and precision of a pro race car driver, and shut off the engine. "When we get home, I want you to look up Adam Clayton Powell Jr. You will learn a lot."

"Mom, don't say it. Please," I begged. "I have so much homework."

"Well, add this to your homework. This is what college life is about. You have to study and get assignments done in whatever time you have."

"But I'm not in college until next year."

"Well, this is good practice then. Write me a paper on Adam Clayton Powell Jr."

I wanted to scream. I didn't have time for additional research projects. Since I was a kid, every time I didn't know about something or gave a wrong answer, my mother would make me do a research paper about it.

And people wondered how I knew so much about so many random things.

"Now stop pouting, because I'm not going to change my mind, and you know it. Let me run into the post office really quick, and I'll meet you next door."

"I still don't understand why we can't just have our mail delivered to our house like everyone else does."

"That's because I'm trying to keep us off the grid," my mom joked and planted a kiss on my cheek.

The kiss softened me. A little. "How about I get the drinks and meet you back here?" I asked.

"Oh, you're treating?"

"Well, not exactly. Technically, my money is your money because you gave it to me. So . . . kind of?"

She grinned. "Works for me."

We hopped out of the car and exchanged fist bumps as we passed each other. Mom hurried into the post office while I went to the shop beside it, stopping to hold the door for a lady juggling a stroller and a latte.

"Aren't you just the sweetest?" she said with a smile. "Thanks so much."

"You're welcome," I replied. *See, not racist at all.*

"You can go ahead," she said when I joined the line behind her. "I don't know what I want yet."

"Thanks," I said and stepped up to the counter.

"Welcome to Pacific Table. What'll you have today, Storm?"

"Bryson, can you stop saying my name when I come in? You make it seem like I'm here every day, and not like we go to school together."

He laughed. "The usual? Two dairy-free pineapple bubble teas with strawberry pearls?"

"Yep. It's perfection."

"Can I convince you to try the mango today?"

"You could try, but I prefer to keep my taste buds on famil-iar grounds, thank you very much."

"All right. I'll have that right up for you, pretty lady."

I blushed as I moved to the other end of the counter. Bryson was always flirty, but I could never tell if it was just his friendly work demeanor or if there was something more to it.

Behind me, a couple about my age were in a heated conversation at a window-side table. I stole a quick glance, then caught sight of my mother huffing outside and flapping open a red envelope like it was her worst enemy. After she read the card, she shoved the envelope into her coat pocket, returned to the car, and placed the rest of the mail on the dashboard.

"Here ya go, Storm." Bryson said as he slid the drinks across the counter.

"Thanks, Bryson. See you in class. Must be nice to only do half-days at school."

"I don't know how nice it is, but at least I get to work more hours so I can save up for college in the fall."

I nodded. *The fall.* My mind went back to my dream. How could we possibly think of the future when the world was going to end.

"Storm . . . are you okay?"

I snapped out of my thoughts and gave him a reassuring smile. "Yeah, just a lot on my mind. See you later." I clenched my jaw and turned to leave.

"Hey, don't forget your straws."

"Oh," I said and reached for them. Bryson gently grasped my hand.

Oh my gosh, he's about to ask me out in front of the other customers. *Keep it together, Storm,* I told myself and held my breath.

"Your friend Teresa . . . She's a good girl like you," he said. "She might want to steer clear of Pool."

"Oh—uh—I'll tell her." I laughed nervously, not sure what else to say. "Thanks for the heads up," I said as I backed away.

Bryson nodded and returned to the register to take the next customer's order.

I walked outside and got in the car, then sat there for a moment, holding the cups. *Why did he say that? What in the world happened the other night?*

"Storm!" my mom screamed at me from outside the car, her voice muted. "What are you doing?" She waved her hands at the window, a panicked expression scrawled across her face.

Confused, I looked over to see a random dude sitting in the driver's seat, his eyes bulging at me. "Um . . . You're in the wrong car."

I glanced at the dashboard, then at the floor. Where was my backpack? Mortified, I fiddled with the doorknob as my mom and I simultaneously opened it. "Sorry about that," I told the man and ran around to the passenger side of my *actual* car.

"Storm—"

"Mom, before you go in on me, in my defense, both cars are black and you have to admit, his car looks practically identical to Betty."

"But what were you thinking—I mean, what's on your mind? Is it about writing that paper?"

"Oh, here," I said, handing over her cup and straw. "I was just talking to Bryson..."

"Well, when you came out, your expression looked like you had seen a ghost. What did he say? Are they closing down the shop or something? I hope not, because it's the only place to get bubble tea and ramen in town. But that's not enough for you to confuse someone else's car with ours." She started the engine and backed out of the parking space.

"No, this girl I know is hanging out with the wrong crowd. He must have seen them or something."

My mom's tone softened. "Is she okay?"

"I don't know. I'm concerned about her."

She sipped her tea and interrupted me with a loud burp.

I laughed. "Really, Mom?"

"Eww . . . Excuse me."

"Did you eat salami today?" I asked as I placed my tea in the cup holder, gathered the mail from the dashboard, and straightened it into a stack.

"Actually, that's lasagna you're smelling," she replied with a snicker.

"At least it took the elevator instead of the trash shoot," I replied. It was a gross conversation, but it lightened my mood, and we laughed about farts all the way home.

And I acted like I didn't notice the corner of the red envelope sticking out of her pocket.

11

— · —

My mother could totally have a YouTube channel. It would be called something like "Drama in Scrubs," and I would film and edit it.

Most days, she came home after her shift and either took a quick power nap or proceeded to fill me in on the latest hospital drama—who was let go, who was dating who, or funny things that her patients or their families did that day. Of course, the stories were nothing without her over-the-top reenactments. It's like watching a one-woman comedy show in our living room.

I'm pretty sure she does it just to make me laugh. But even when I'm upset, I get so caught up in her stories that everything else falls away.

While she went to the living room, sipping her bubble tea, I hung up my coat, took my backpack upstairs, and waited to see which mom I would get: Nap Mom or Story Mom?

From my ensuite, I heard her humming as she climbed the stairs. Shortly after, she headed back downstairs yelling,

"Storm, I can't make this stuff up. You will never guess what happened today!"

"Hold that thought," I yelled back. I left the bathroom, leaned over my desk, and opened my laptop. It whirred as it came to life. I typed *Adam Clayton Powell Jr.* in the search engine, then bookmarked a couple of sites to visit later as I finished my tea. "Here I come!"

My feet barely made a sound as I stepped down our worn carpeted steps. Before I made it to the landing, I stopped and leaned over the wooden banister, looking into the living room. The shade was drawn, and the dim light from the corner lamp illuminated more of the ceiling than the room. The news droned softly from the television, blending into the quiet.

Mom was sprawled across the couch, one leg carelessly extended across the top, a sock half falling off her foot. One arm was tucked behind her head, her phone glued to her hand.

"Raincheck on story time, I guess," I mumbled and backed up to the coat hook, watching her snore ever so lightly as I checked the pockets of her quilted bomber coat. The red envelope was gone. *What did she do with it?* I crept around the entire first floor, rummaging through drawers and probing the trash. Zilch.

Next, I went upstairs and poked around my mother's bedroom, trying to determine where the envelope would be.

She'd brought it inside, and it wasn't in any trash bin. Why would she hide it?

Maybe she'd hidden it under her perfectly fluffed pillows? Or tucked it away under her not-so-secret stash of chocolate? If it was a late Valentine's Day card, who would've sent it? She said there were no prospects in Spencer.

My mother's bed was meticulously made, and the faint scent of lavender lingered in the air from the scented candle on her nightstand. In the car, I had playfully asked if the mail included a fat check from some rich uncle, even though I wasn't aware of any long-lost relatives.

"Just bills and junk, as usual," she'd nonchalantly replied. The woman who always quoted Proverbs 6:16, "God hates a lying tongue," lied to me. But why? Bills weren't shipped in red envelopes, and if it was junk mail, she wouldn't have kept it.

After snooping through my mother's nightstand drawers, I moved on to her walk-in closet. Her shoes were stacked high on shelves, each pair encased in a box. If she hid it in one of those, I was in trouble. I would have to check every single box, and that could take forever.

I glanced up at the gray cube perched on the highest shelf. If she were going to hide something from me, why not there? She knew I loathed guns. But little did my mother know, I had discovered the key to her gun safe in her medicine cabinet months ago.

I retrieved the key and lifted the safe from the shelf. It was surprisingly light. That's because it wasn't a gun safe at all, but a fireproof safe box. *She lied to me about this being a gun safe?* I set it on my Mom's bed, unlocked it, and lifted the lid. There was no gun inside. Instead, atop a stack of countless letters lay the red envelope.

The handwriting on the envelope was in tiny cursive that I could barely read, but it was clearly addressed to Rebecca Davis. I snapped a picture of the return address with my phone and quickly opened the envelope. Inside was a card. On the front was a field of sunflowers under a blue sky. On the inside were two words written in blue ink: *Forgive me.*

12

The overpowering white cotton scented sachets my mom strategically placed in her closet mixed with the aftertaste of the pineapple bubble tea on my tongue, creating a concoction that made my stomach churn.

I turned the envelope over and tried to read the scrawled return address written on the seal flap. My heartbeat raced, an involuntary reaction to a fear I couldn't understand, and a cascade of questions flooded my mind. *Why wasn't this a gun safe? Why hide letters? Why did someone want her to forgive them?*

Suddenly, I froze. What caught my attention was the hushed silence as the television shut off, accompanied by my mom's waking sounds—a soft "Umm . . ." that I fondly referred to as her "music."

I panicked and clumsily tried to shove the card back into the envelope. Finally, it slid in. I tossed it inside the safe and locked it before hoisting it onto the top shelf. Mom's footsteps were coming up the stairs, and there was no way I could escape her room before she reached the hallway.

I stared at the key in my hand before hastily stuffing it into my pocket. I considered turning off the closet light and pretending to wait there to scare her. *No, I haven't done that in years. Now she's going to catch me and not trust me anymore. Why did I have to go snooping around?*

Just as I made up my mind to walk back to my bedroom, she sauntered down the hallway and disappeared into her ensuite. That was my chance to tiptoe out of the closet, but what if she had already looked for me in my room?

A couple of minutes passed before she emerged from the bathroom and walked over to her closet. "Stormie? What are you doing?" she asked with hands on her hips.

I sat on the floor with three of her shoe boxes around me, strapping a pair of her four-inch pumps to my feet. "Trying to figure out which pair I want to wear to prom," I replied with a mischievous grin.

She laughed. "You? In heels? That's a disaster waiting to happen."

I laughed, too—a nervous laugh. "That's why I need practice."

She gasped and held her chest. "Oh, I know what happened—the reason you got in the wrong car! It was Bryson!

Did he ask you to prom? That boy is a catch. Well, he seems like it anyway."

"Here, help me up," I said, extending a hand toward her. "And no, he didn't ask me."

She steadied me as I stood. "Take it slow. Oh, and just so you know, you're not going to wear out my heels practicing for the dance. We'll get you a cheap pair from the Dollar Store."

I giggled. "Since when does the Dollar Store sell high heels? The thought of that concerns me."

I continued down the hall and Mom watched my efforts with a mixture of amusement and worry as I wobbled unsteadily in her shoes.

"How's that? I've got it, right?"

"Not bad, Stormie," she said, following a couple feet behind and keeping her arms primed to catch me if I stumbled.

"I'm too sexy for myself, too sexy for myself," I sang as I swayed my hips and made her laugh.

The initial excitement of discovering the envelope quickly faded as I stood before the woman who'd been nothing but incredibly supportive and proud of me. The good girl in me called me out for snooping in my mother's things, the guilt lingering like the aftertaste of a chalky aspirin.

I carefully walked back to her closet—slow, deliberate steps. I don't know what happened when I got there, but I wobbled like the scarecrow in *The Wizard of Oz* and held onto a shelf to keep from falling. A domino effect ensued. Shoeboxes came tumbling down around me.

"At least I thought you had it," my mom said, staring at the pile on the floor.

We both laughed, momentarily easing the tension inside me. For a split second, I considered confessing and telling her what I found. But I quickly dismissed the idea because, well, I rarely listened to my brain in these matters.

With a sheepish grin, I slid my finger beneath the strap and slipped off one of the shoes. "Maybe I should stick to flats for prom."

"That's not a bad idea. But remember, it's going to depend on the dress, which we haven't even begun to look for yet."

"Well, if I'm going alone, I'm wearing a girl tux. A white one."

"What the heck is that?"

"A woman's tuxedo. I saw Blake Lively wearing one online."

"Where do you come up with these things? That's a hard no, Storm."

"Mom, my prom, my choice."

"My credit card," she replied.

She had a point. I put her shoes back where I found them, and we exited the room together, the red envelope's secrets still tucked away in that box.

Back in my bedroom, I slipped on my cozy socks with rubber grips on the bottom, then remembered the safe key in my pocket that I still needed to put back in the medicine cabinet.

While my mom headed downstairs to blend her pre-workout shake, I put the key back in her medicine cabinet and then went to my bedroom and scrolled to the photo of the red envelope on my phone. *What the heck does "Forgive me" mean?* Then I noticed the empty bubble tea cup on my desk and I thought of Bryson's comment about Teresa. *Why is she ignoring my calls?*

Once again, I tried phoning her and mentally rehearsed the message I would leave on her voicemail. *Hey, girl. It's me again. Still trying to get a hold of you. Why aren't you picking up or calling me back? You're treating me like I'm Tiffany Lancaster!*

"Hello?"

"T-bird?"

I couldn't believe she actually picked up. T-bird was a nickname I had given Teresa in middle school. I thought if I used it, it might lighten the mood.

"Hey, Storm," she replied, her voice raspy.

I stood at my window, fixated on the squirrels darting across the branches of an oak tree, one of them defying gravity. I read somewhere that squirrels had swiveling ankle joints, allowing them to climb and hang in various positions. Then I pictured myself rotating my feet 180-degrees like a squirrel.

Nope. That's Gross.

"Storm?"

"I'm here. Sorry, did I wake you?" I asked and sat at the end of my bed.

"No, I'm up. I just haven't spoken much today. What's going on?"

"Have you checked your messages or your texts?"

"I've been kind of avoiding any human interaction. But yeah . . ."

All she says is "yeah" when I've been calling and texting since last night?

"Okay," I replied slowly. "I just wanted to make sure you were—uh, you weren't at school today. Are you feeling all right?" I hesitated, unsure of how to bring up what Bryson said, about her not hanging out with Pool, or Todd's comment about her being "wasted."

Teresa sighed heavily. "To be honest, no. I just needed a mental health day, you know?"

Instead of speaking, I stood and slowly paced. When you don't know what to say, it's best to say nothing. So, I waited, hoping it would prompt her to say more.

"I stayed home because my head was spinning."

That actually worked? "Because of your hangover?" *Oops . . . did I say that out loud?*

"Who told you that?"

I lightly knocked my fist against my forehead a few times before answering. "It's all over the school."

"That's just great. I can't believe everyone knows about it already," Teresa groaned. "I was afraid of this, that's why I turned off my phone. Figures . . . People love turning everything into gossip."

"Are you okay?" I asked, genuinely concerned.

"I don't even know. But this will all blow over eventually and someone else will become the newest target of senior year gossip, right?" Teresa tried to sound convincing, but her voice quivered. "I'm just so embarrassed about everything that went down at that swamp party. And then, to make matters worse, finding out there are pictures and videos circulating . . . I just want to disappear."

My jaw practically hit the floor. "There are? You've seen them?"

"Unfortunately. Before I shut my phone off."

"Who took them?"

"No clue, but Tiffany Lancaster posted them."

"Teresa, I'm so sorry this is happening to you. But I haven't seen them, and if I haven't, then maybe not everyone has. Do your parents know?"

"No."

"You should tell them. They can talk to the principal, and he will make Tiffany take them down."

"No, I can't do that. Storm, my parents can't see those photos. They have this perfect image of me. I can't let them see me as anything other than their darling little girl."

She had a point. We attended the same church, and Teresa's parents were always front and center, beaming, whenever she did anything on the pulpit—whether she was reading the weekly announcements or belting out off-key hymns with the youth praise team. They looked at her like she was the brightest star on stage, their darling little girl who could do no wrong.

That's why I wondered why they allowed their precious baby girl to show off her tatas in those tight shirts she wore to school.

I was dying to ask her what was on the videos but decided against it. "They're your parents, they will love you no matter what," I reasoned.

"Not when it comes to something like this. They'll be disappointed and ashamed; I just know it."

"Well, darling little girl or not, you should tell them. Then they can go *John Wick* on Tiffany's butt and make her get rid of the photos. What do your parents think was wrong with you today?"

Teresa lowered her voice. "They think I got food poisoning from eating too many spicy tacos last night. Hey, I've gotta go. I think I'm going to throw up again."

The call dropped and I flung my phone onto my bed like a hot potato. *That's too much drama. I sure wouldn't want to switch places with her, and I bet she wished she hadn't gone to that party.* I glanced at my phone. *Should I text her? Give her space? She must feel so alone . . .*

A part of me said it wasn't my problem, but a tiny Christian voice inside said "WWJD?"

Fine. Fine! I reluctantly typed out a message: *T-bird, hang in there. I'm here if you need anything. Even if it means handing out slaps at school.* I hoped that part would make her laugh.

As I waited for a response, I scrolled through Tiffany Lancaster's social media profiles. The pictures and videos were making the rounds, each one more cringe-worthy and embarrassing than the next. Faces twisted in laughter and shock, fingers pointing, and phones held up to capture the moment. The comments section was filled with emojis and cruel statements. It was like watching a wildfire spreading.

This was way more than gossip. Tiffany was trying to humiliate her.

Half an hour later, my phone buzzed with a text: *Thanks, Storm. I'm freaking out over this whole Tiffany situation. Maybe I should try talking to her about deleting those posts. But what if she refuses?*

Me: *Are you crazy? You're dealing with Tiffany Lancaster. She won't care about your feelings. You need to bring in the big guns—your counselor or the principal. They might be able to intervene and handle it discreetly.*

There was a brief pause before Teresa replied: *I guess it's worth a shot. Please tell me you'll come with me. I don't think I can face this alone.*

I gulped, rereading her text. *What? She's got other friends. Who said anything about—* I knew what a good girl should say or was expected to say, but I couldn't. I sighed and texted: *Honestly, Teresa, I was only trying to make sure you're okay. I'm not interested in getting any further involved in school drama.*

As I pressed send, I began to feel anxious about a problem that wasn't even mine. *Not my circus, not my monkeys.* "Plus, the Bible says to mind your business," I reminded myself.

Teresa responded: *Excuse me, but didn't you say you were here if I needed anything?*

Me: *Yeah, like if you needed to talk or help with homework or something.*

Teresa: *Really, Storm?*

I didn't respond. She wasn't going to lay a guilt trip on me for a something *she* got herself into. *The fallout of that situation is going to be crazy. I'm not getting involved in that. Note to self: never offer support without specifying which kind.*

My laptop hummed to life as if I had tapped on the keyboard. I sat at my desk, determined to start and finish the paper on Adam Clayton Powell Jr. that night. But thinking about the paper got me thinking about the red envelope.

Again, I pulled up the photo of it on my phone.

Seriously though, none of this will even matter when the world ends.

14

—·—

The full moon hung low in the night sky, casting long, eerie shadows that danced in the wind. The air was thick with tension and the scent of impending rain, a stark contrast to the warm glow emanating from the rustic cabin nestled amidst the towering oaks. I watched from outside of it all, seeing the crackling fire inside the cabin illuminate two figures: one hunched over in an armchair, his face hidden in the shadow from the brim of his fedora hat, and the other a woman, near the window, her silhouette reflected in the glass.

Blonde hair and green eyes. The woman was me.

The two were motionless, and the occasional pop from the burning wood of the fireplace was the only sound. Finally, she turned to face the man and a red envelope dropped from his hand to the floor. Her voice—*my* voice—cut through the silence like a knife. "You've come a long way to find me. What do you want?"

"To tell you of what is to come."

It was a different scene, but the same dream once again. A warning of the fate of the world. This time, I awoke with my heart pounding, not screaming like a banshee, and realized that I got closer to seeing the man's face. *Why did he have the envelope?*

But the dream wasn't what woke me. I was startled awake by the creaking sound of my bedroom window opening. I scrambled back against my headboard, searching frantically for something to grab and hit the intruder with. *Go into attack mode, Storm. Just start swinging before they can even get inside!* But my body wouldn't listen to my brain.

The window rose, and just as I was about to scream loud enough to be heard clear across town, Kendra's braids cascaded into view, and she climbed inside.

"What are you doing here?" I whisper-yelled.

"Visiting you."

"You couldn't just ring the doorbell like a normal human being?"

Another head came through the window, and I jumped again.

"Hey, Storm," said Raine.

I pulled my blanket up to my neck. "Can you lower your voice?" Thank goodness I was wearing flannel pajama bottoms and a T-shirt, because who knows what kind of embarrassing sleepwear I could have been caught in.

Stumbling out of bed, I inched my door open and peeked down the hall. My mom's bedroom door was closed, and the noise machine she used at night was blaring. Phew. That was a relief.

I closed my door and noticed my nightlight's failed attempt to light up anything more than a foot away. The fairy lights behind my bed weren't doing much better.

Raine lounged in the corner chair hanging from my ceiling, watching me with a mischievous grin. Meanwhile, Kendra sat on the windowsill, looking unconcerned.

"Ha! Called it," exclaimed Raine, triumphantly pointing at the wall behind my bed. "You have a mural. Wow. You did your thing."

I rolled my eyes. "Congratulations, Sherlock. And thanks. Now why the heck are you two here?"

Raine tilted his head to the left, then to the right, still examining my mural. "Oh snap. I see what you did. Those flowers are actually lungs. That's cool."

I glanced at my wall, impressed that he noticed, but tried to keep up my indifferent persona.

"I know you've done a self-portrait. Where is it?" he asked, looking around.

"Why are you acting like this is some casual visit?"

"I bet that will teach you to start locking your window," said Kendra.

I clicked on the reading light beside my bed. "I didn't think anyone would ever actually climb up here. It's not even a real balcony, it's only decorative."

Raine glanced behind the chair as he rocked. "But I didn't expect a chalkboard wall with equations scribbled all over it." He turned back to me. "You go to bed too early."

"I'm in AP Calculus. And, for your information, studies have shown that people who get fewer than six hours of sleep experience one point five times more asthma attacks than those who sleep seven to nine hours," I replied matter-of-factly.

Raine turned to Kendra with a raised eyebrow. "Does she always throw out random facts? 'Studies have shown' this and that?"

Kendra nodded. "All. The. Time." She clapped with each word.

I grabbed her hands. "Stop clapping. Don't you know how to be quiet?"

"That could work for the show," Raine continued.

"Both of you just stop." I pointed at Raine. "I told you I'm not doing the show, with your hashtag rizz persuasiveness."

"Is she speaking in hashtags? Don't do that. It's weird. But thanks for the compliment. I don't think anyone has called me charismatic before."

That earned him an eye roll. I turned to Kendra and crossed my arms. "I'm mad at you, so both of you need to get out of my house. Right now. Climb back down the way you came."

"Sheesh, she's grumpy when she doesn't get her rest. She'll be all right," said Kendra. "Ignore that."

"Stop talking like I'm not here."

"Anyway, you didn't return my texts this afternoon, and Raine told me what went down after school, so I knew you were mad. We came here to squash this."

I leaned against my desk. "Why couldn't we discuss this tomorrow?"

"Because we're recording the podcast tomorrow," said Raine.

"We who?"

Raine huffed. "I already apologized."

"I'm sorry, too," said Kendra. "It was just a joke. Raine didn't think you would talk to him again without me. I think you'll regret it if you don't try the podcast thing."

They both studied me, waiting for me to say something. And I wished I could come up with some clever comeback. But then I thought of Teresa and the litany of texts I sent her that day and how I kind of reneged on helping her.

What are you doing, Storm? You said you didn't want to get involved, my mind reminded me.

But I ignored it, as usual. "Will you still allow me to talk about absolutely anything I want to talk about?"

Raine sat forward, steadying the swing. "Cross my heart. No censorship. Are you in?"

"Unlock your phone and let me see it."

"Why?"

"Just do it, idiot," said Kendra.

Raine handed over his phone, and I scrolled through his texts from Kendra. There were no photos of me. Then I went through his photo gallery.

"Not one of you. Satisfied? Do you believe us now?" asked Raine.

I pointed at his phone. "Who took these pictures? Did you? Were you there?"

"What is it?" Kendra asked, moving closer to get a better look.

"It's Teresa."

15

Kendra's eyes were wide and unblinking, mirroring mine. Her breaths hitched as we scrolled through the images of Teresa. Our friend who laughed too loudly and cared too much about everything and everyone, reduced to this. It was clear that someone had been following her, documenting her every move.

"Were you there?" I questioned again.

Raine's eyes bulged, and he shook his head. "No. I promise you; I didn't take those photos. I have no idea who did, but I can tell you this, they are being sent to *everybody*. I'm surprised you two haven't gotten them yet."

"On your mama?" asked Kendra.

"Heck no. But I swear on my collection of vinyl records."

Kendra snatched the phone from my hands and examined the pictures herself, her brows furrowing in concern. "This changes things," she muttered under her breath. "What is that?"

I squinted at the screen, then gasped. "Oh my gosh. Those are panties. Who stuck the phone under her skirt?"

"I can't," said Kendra, shoving the phone into Raine's hands. "I am thoroughly disgusted."

Raine stared blankly at the photo, seemingly deep in thought. I got the feeling he wasn't actually seeing it. Then, he pointed at the phone. "I say we use this on the podcast. We can talk about how messed up something like this is, without mentioning names."

Kendra and I exchanged glances. The discussion would be an invasion of privacy, but it was the reason I said I would do the podcast. On the one hand, it could raise awareness about underage drinking. On the other, it could exacerbate the situation, exposing Teresa to even more scrutiny and unwanted attention. "I don't know," I said hesitantly. "We have to think about the consequences. What if this only adds fuel to the fire? This girl is suffering right now."

"How do you know? Did you talk to her?" asked Kendra.

"Yes, tonight."

Raine nodded slowly. "You're right. We'd have to handle it delicately."

"What else did she—" As Kendra spoke, my bedroom door opened.

"Kendra?" said my mom with a yawn. "What are you doing here at this hour?"

Kendra and I exchanged panicked looks. *Please don't turn around*, I silently begged. The swing moved, and before my mother could turn to look in that direction, Raine slid behind the door.

"Mom, how about some hot chocolate?" I blurted out, trying to distract her.

"It's too late for sugar," she responded, eyeing Kendra suspiciously.

Kendra glanced at me, and I gave her my shrug face, squinting and lifting one brow higher than the other.

"My dad and I got into it," Kendra confessed, eyes darting between me and my mother. "I just needed to talk to someone—in person. I'm heading out now."

"Do you want a ride?" She began to turn toward her room. "Let me throw on something."

"No, that's okay. He'll be mad that I woke you. My bike is outside."

Mom studied her. "I don't know . . ."

"I promise I'll text as soon as I get home."

"Mom, it's just around the corner. If she goes through the backyard, she'll be there in three minutes."

Kendra's phone buzzed with a text, and she quickly glanced at the screen. "That's my dad. He wants me to meet him outside. I'll bike down to the corner." She shuffled past my mother and headed downstairs.

"Mom, I'll see her out," I said, stopping her from following Kendra. At the front door, I tapped my ear and pointed up.

Kendra gave a slight nod, signaling that she understood my mother was listening. "Later," she said before I shut the door behind her.

That was close. I let out a huge sigh of relief as I closed my eyes and leaned against the door.

My eyes shot open. *Raine is still up there!* And my mom was probably still in my bedroom. I dashed up the stairs, taking them two at a time while trying not to trip over my own feet, and stopped abruptly when I saw her peering down at me from the landing.

"Is she okay?"

"Just some typical Kendra drama." I could feel my face reddening. I was a terrible liar, and in the last twenty-four hours, I had told more lies than I had all year. Before she could ask anything else, I faked a long, hard yawn and covered my mouth. "I'm exhausted," I said through my hand. "Good-night, Mom."

"Goodnight, Stormie," she replied and headed back down the hall. As she walked across the threshold to her room, I closed my bedroom door.

Raine was still behind it.

I held a finger to my lips and shut off the light. We stood there, listening to each other breathe. Then my phone buzzed.

Raine: *Not going to risk talking. That was me texting Kendra. Glad it worked. We'll pick this up tomorrow at school.*

His shadowy figure loomed by my window, and I wondered if he could see me any better than I could see him. He slowly opened it, trying not to make a sound, and stepped one leg over the sill, then the other. With a wave, he was off, climbing down the side of my house. I closed the window and watched him disappear below the trees.

As I crawled into bed, the events of the night created a mixture of excitement and nerves that swirled around in my stomach like a hurricane. The sheets felt cool against my skin, providing a stark contrast to the heat of my sweaty palms. I closed my eyes and tried to push away my thoughts, but there were so many what ifs.

What if I had gotten caught with Raine in my bedroom? And in the middle of the night? How did he remain so still that my mother didn't notice him there?

After turning onto my side and hugging my pillow, I whispered into the darkness, "What am I getting myself into?"

16

—·—

The front of the school was bustling as usual as I got out of old Betty and waved goodbye to my mother.

Dodging the crowd, I walked across the lawn, passing the senior grid. That's when I noticed Teresa sitting in her mother's emerald green Prius. It was understandable that she had driven her mother's car rather than allow herself to be trapped on a school bus with everyone staring her down and talking about her.

Her head rested against the steering wheel like a wilting flower, and for a moment, I thought she was out cold. But when I tapped on the window, she glanced up and nodded. I couldn't tell if she'd been sleeping, praying, or just trying to calm her nerves. All I knew was that she seemed relieved to see me, like she had been waiting for someone to save her from her thoughts or to give her a nudge to step out of the car.

The dark circles under her eyes made her look sickly. She probably hadn't slept much. I didn't know if she was still upset about my text, but she mustered a small smile when she saw me.

"Hey, Storm," she said as she dragged herself out of the car and grabbed her backpack out of the backseat. "I was just psyching myself up to face everybody."

To my surprise, she didn't seem the slightest bit mad at me. But that's how Teresa was. In my book, she was truly a good person.

She adjusted her backpack on her shoulder, and I noticed she wasn't wearing one of her fitted shirts, but an oversized sweatshirt like I might wear.

I offered a sympathetic nod. "Let's face 'em together."

She hesitated. "Are you sure you want to be seen with me?"

"Of course. Listen, that was just one night. It doesn't define you. In a few months, high school will be over. All of this will be a fleeting memory once you head off to college. Don't let this get to you like it's life ending or anything."

Inside, all I could think was, *Girl, that was good. Where did that come from?*

Teresa's face lit up with relief. "Yeah, I'll be going to Full Sail University in Florida."

"Cool. Am I the first to know?"

"Besides, my parents? Yes."

She shut the car door, and, together, we walked toward Beacon High's main entrance. Heads turned as we strolled past the groups outside, then whispers trailed us in the halls. Teresa stared straight ahead, clutching a textbook to her chest as if it were a shield or talisman protecting her from the world. I knew that book was the only thing keeping her from breaking down. She squeezed it so tightly that her knuckles were white.

We pushed through, ignoring the sideways glances, until one jerk had to make a snide remark, "There's the drunk I was looking for. Oh, I guess you're sober now?"

I thought Teresa was going to crumble to the floor. I grabbed her arm and led her to Mrs. Fisher, the school counselor who happened to be Teresa's favorite. I prayed she could offer Teresa some form of help.

As we entered her office, Mrs. Fisher quickly spooned the last of her yogurt into her mouth, dropped the container and plastic spoon in the trash, and greeted us warmly. Beside her, the wall was littered with flyers, sticky notes, and senior photos. One of those photos, hanging at an angle in the center, was of Teresa—outside somewhere, wearing a white strapless gown. She looked like a Disney princess.

Mrs. Fisher noticed Teresa's distress immediately. "Is everything okay?"

Teresa's lip quivered as she struggled to speak. "No. Everything sucks."

Mrs. Fisher motioned for us to take a seat on the couch and settled into her chair across from us as she moved loose strands of auburn hair behind her ears. "What's going on?" she asked gently.

Teresa hesitated, prompting Mrs. Fisher to glance at me.

"I'm just here for support. Tell her, Teresa."

Teresa slowly unraveled the events of the party: the blurry memories, Tiffany capturing pictures and videos without her consent, and the rapid spread of the compromising content throughout the school. She showed Mrs. Fisher some of the posts on social media, before going into a full-on ugly cry.

"I see," Mrs. Fisher said after a moment of silence. "Thank you for bringing this to my attention."

That's it? "What can she do to make them stop?" I asked.

Mrs. Fisher's eyes were fixed on Teresa. Her brow furrowed. "Unfortunately, there is not much we can do about what has already been posted online. But I can have a chat with Tiffany and ask her to take them down."

"But what if she refuses?" Teresa asked.

"We will cross that bridge when we get there. But, FYI, we take cyber bullying very seriously," Mrs. Fisher said with a re-assuring smile. "For now, I suggest you ignore the comments and reactions online and here at school. It might be a good idea to stay off of social media altogether for a while."

"Easier said than done," I muttered, then rose from the couch and headed toward the door.

Teresa followed me out of the office. "Thanks, Mrs. Fisher."

I walked Teresa to class—not as her bodyguard or anything. I just figured she wasn't ready to face the hordes of students alone. Not yet.

"Listen, don't go to the cafeteria or courtyard today."

"I hadn't planned on it."

"Good. Trust me, this is going to blow over quickly. Before you know it, it will be old news." I gave her an encouraging grin. "See you later. Text if you need me to beat someone up."

A slight grin tugged at Teresa's lips. "You? No way. I wouldn't let you tarnish your good girl reputation like that."

"Did I say me? Oh, I meant Kendra."

"That's more like it," Teresa said and slipped into her classroom.

My smile faded. I felt bad for thinking it, but man, I was glad I wasn't her.

17

Kendra plopped down beside me at lunch, her tray over-flowing with crispy fries. "You know you can't stay mad at me."

"Who said I was?" I asked coolly as I snagged a fry. "This is ridiculous—look at this potato mountain. They shouldn't allow you to buy so many. Don't come whining to me when you start breaking out from all of this grease. And how late did you get to school this morning?"

"Girl, don't even ask. I couldn't wake up. My dad practically had to drag me out of bed. He's threatening to install a shock collar."

"And your shirt is on backwards."

"No, it's not."

"It is. I have the same one."

"Dang it!" Kendra exclaimed, feeling for the label under her braids.

I tapped Kendra's leg, and she followed my gaze. Tiffany Lancaster strutted past us with a smug grin, reveling in the chaos she'd created.

"Where is Teresa?" Kendra asked as she gathered her front braids into a high ponytail and secured them with a scrunchie.

"Library or computer lab. She won't come in here today. Maybe not for a while."

"Can you blame her?"

"Nope. Oh, you're coming with me to do the podcast thing, right?"

"Do I have a choice? My bed is calling me."

"You owe me."

"I was joking. Of course. I've got you, Storm. I just need to—"

"Turn your shirt around?"

"Heck no. It's been backward all day, so it's going to stay that way."

I didn't see Teresa again that day, but I heard she got called to the principal's office. That might explain why.

After school, Kendra met me at my locker and then took me to the podcast studio, a small room tucked in the back corner of the school library. No one else was there yet, so we dropped our bags and settled into the two seats behind the microphones.

"Put those on," Kendra said as she pointed.

I picked up the headphones from the table and adjusted them on my head.

"Hello, listeners," Kendra said into the mic. "Welcome back to another stinkin' crazy episode of The Storm and Kendra Show!"

I grinned at her.

"We're here to discuss the recent incident involving Tiffany Lancaster," she began, just as Raine stormed into the room and shut the door behind him.

He stopped mid-stride. "Glad you've made yourself comfortable, Storm. Kendra, get out from behind there. You do know, nothing is turned on yet, right?"

"Relax. I was just warming everything up for you," she replied and removed her headphones.

Raine took off his jacket. "How are you doing, Storm? Are you ready?"

"I guess so. I had no idea this room was inside the library. This is like, legit."

"Yup," he said as he fiddled with buttons and cords. Another guy walked in and started helping him. "This is Rick."

"Hey," Rick said without looking up from what he was doing.

A few minutes later, Raine sat down beside me and pushed the long curls from his face. "Don't be nervous."

I must have looked it. My palms were certainly sweating.

"Speak into the mic."

"What?"

"We have to test it," Raine explained, sliding on his headphones, which also served as a headband to hold back his hair. "Testing one, two," he said into the mic, then gestured for me to do the same.

"Testing one, two," I repeated awkwardly.

"Louder."

I raised my voice and stole a glance at Kendra. She smirked and gave me a thumbs up. My clammy hands gripped the table on either side of the mic.

Raine grabbed my hand and squeezed it briefly before letting go. "Ready?"

I nodded, anxiously tapping my feet. *About as ready as I'll ever be.*

"All right, we're live in three . . . two . . . one," said the Rick. Then he pointed at us. A red recording light blinked, signaling we were on air.

"I'm the bad boy, Raine, and I want to introduce you to my new co-host, Storm."

He nudged me with his elbow, and I forced out a squeaky, "Hey there." I cringed at how lame I sounded.

"She's a woman of few words. For now. We're just two unlikely friends bringing you this week's podcast. Welcome to Things We Don't Tell Our Parents: Uncensored, streaming on SpotOver and FIcast, where we discuss how to survive high school: From the drama and the homework to the friends and the enemies, and all the hilarious moments in between—we've got you covered."

He lifted a hand toward me to add in whatever I wanted to say, but I was speechless. The words were there, but my vocal cords were holding them hostage and wouldn't let them out. I shook my head.

"Just remember, we're also filming this," Raine said, pointing to the camera a few feet in front of us that I failed to notice them set up.

"Wait, what? As in *video*?" I gasped, frantically smoothing my hair and attempting to straighten out my crumpled sweatshirt.

"Yep," Rain replied.

"Now you tell me."

"Don't worry, you look great. And that's not an exaggeration, she's naturally beautiful."

I'm pretty sure I turned red.

"So, Storm, what's your take on senior year? Are you pumped or nah?"

I stared at the mic and glanced at Kendra leaning against the black styrofoam wall, arms crossed. Her eyes were on me, silently daring me to bring up Teresa. Instead, my mind went blank, and I blurted out, "Hey, do you guys like Queen?"

Raine had been taking a sip from a water flask and almost choked. "Queen? As in the band? That's, like . . . random."

"I just asked because that's what your name means."

"Are you serious? Somebody look it up. I need proof that this girl isn't messing with me, acting like she doesn't know what to say and then drops my name's origin on me."

The guy in charge of the mixing board held up his phone and shouted, "It's legit!"

"There you have it. Why didn't I know that? That's wild, Storm." His finger jabbed in my direction. "I forgot you know a bunch of random stuff. What about yours?"

"Storm means tempest. It's usually a boy's name and is super popular in Denmark and Sweden."

"Wow. Let's do another one. What about Kendra."

"It means knowing."

"Seriously, do you just know the meaning of every person's name?"

"No, I look up the meanings of people's names if I'm associated with them in any way, that's all."

"Well, consider me flattered and impressed. That was a bomb introduction to yourself. So, ask a question, any question, and we'll get into it."

"Okay . . . Before I interview anyone, I ask them one question. The answers I get are always interesting."

I made that up, but Raine looked intrigued. "Okay. Go for it."

I paused dramatically before delivering my question. "If you knew the exact date the world would end, what would you do differently?"

Kendra's mouth dropped.

Raine let out a low whistle. "That's deep."

"I know. And let's say it's ending soon."

"Sheesh, no pressure." Raine swallowed hard, contemplating for a moment. "If I knew the date the world would end, I think I would start living more fearlessly. I would take all the risks I've been too afraid to take and chase after my dreams without hesitation." He stroked his chin thoughtfully. "I'll also add that I would spend more time with the people I love, making each moment count. And I wouldn't waste any more time on things that don't truly matter."

"And what if it turned out that the date was wrong? That the world wasn't really coming to an end?" I asked.

"Plot twist. Cool." Raine shrugged, a playful glint dancing in his eyes. "Then at least I would've lived my best life, right?"

I nodded. "Great answers. But tell me, why aren't you doing those things now? I mean, that's really living, right? Why are you holding back?"

We locked eyes for a long moment before Raine slowly grinned. "Hang on now, you gotta answer first. What would *you* do if you knew the world was ending?"

I took a deep breath, choosing my response carefully. "If I knew the date the world would end," I began slowly, "I would call out every bully in the school and make them apologize to everyone they've ever wronged." *There. I said it. At least I didn't use names.*

Raine's grin grew wider. He knew where I was going. "Do tell. What kind of stuff have they done? What have you heard?"

"I've heard about wild parties, underage drinking, and all sorts of stuff."

"At Beacon High? Shocking." There was no surprise in his voice.

"You know, I've always heard that hurt people hurt people. And it's messed up."

"I agree, and I'll tell you something—I've heard stories about kids being hurt because of gossip, and if you are one of the people spreading those stories, you are part of the problem.

I couldn't like Raine any more than I did at that moment.

"Here's to being part of the solution," he said and lifted his water flask toward me. I think we both realized at the same time that I didn't bring anything to drink. Thank goodness for Kendra. She tossed me her water bottle, and for once, I caught it.

"To being part of the solution," I replied and bumped Raine's flask.

Kendra flashed a knowing smile.

"Oh, be quiet," I mouthed.

18

—·—

The podcast was uncharted territory for me, totally out of my comfort zone. But when Raine's eyes met mine, I saw in *his* an unspoken challenge—we were pushing boundaries, and he was daring me to enjoy it as much as he did.

An hour passed, then a second. I sat in the rigid chair, headphones clamped over my ears, navigating as best I could as we recorded another episode. Of course, Raine had conveniently failed to mention that they always recorded two at a time. Across the table, Kendra's gaze never wavered, while Raine's infectious energy filled the room as he talked, bouncing in his seat like popcorn in a microwave.

"Until next time, boys and girls," he finally stated. "We're out!"

Some recorded outro message played, and I took the headphones off as Raine did the same.

"That's a wrap," he said and clasped his hands together.

I stood, noticing how quiet he had become. *I sucked. I knew it.* I walked around the table to Kendra with a frown. "How did I do?"

"How did you do?" Raine asked, not allowing her to respond. He ran over and lifted me up in a spinning hug. "You killed it, Storm!" He kissed me hard on the cheek as he set me down. "That was perfect. Sure, we ruffled a few feathers, but we did it the right way. *You* did it the right way. I can't believe it. You're a natural, Storm! Rick, what did you think?"

"She's a keeper, that's for sure."

"I told you. Didn't I tell you?" asked Kendra as she and Raine high-fived.

I barely heard them. I was still reeling from the kiss.

Raine clasped his hands together in front of me and gave me those puppy dog eyes, just like he'd done that first time in the hall. "Please come back. Say you will."

I wasn't sure of what to say, but I had actually enjoyed the talk. It felt good to voice my opinions.

Kendra swooped in with her always-perfect timing, grabbed my hand and proclaimed, "She will!" and pulled me out of the room, barely giving me time to snatch up my backpack.

"The side entrance is the only one unlocked," Rick yelled behind us. I didn't even know how he could see. His hair was so long and hanging in his face.

Then, I froze. "Oh my gosh, I totally forgot to tell my mom. She probably has the National Guard surrounding the building."

"Nah, she's just pulling into the grid. I texted her that you had a debate meeting."

"Why didn't you tell her it was for a podcast?"

"I swear, I have to teach you everything. . . Parents know parents, and depending on what you said today, anything could get back to Teresa's parents. I didn't want to chance it."

I grinned. "How are you so sneaky? Is that innate?"

"Why are you always using big words?" she asked as we walked outside.

"Innate is not a big word."

"Sure, whatever. Oh look, there she is. Can you guys drop me off?"

For the rest of the evening, Raine bombarded me with texts:

Storm, that apocalyptic line was pure genius.

Nice icebreaker. How did you come up with that?

We are going to add that in every episode.

FYI, our listenership is blowing up!

It was all good to hear and I was happy for him, but it also got me thinking. If I truly believed the dream was real, which I did—most of the time, then why wasn't I living *my* best life?

Honestly, I wouldn't even know where to start.

When I got to school the next day, I was met with hordes of "Heys" and grinning faces. *Hmm . . . they must have approved of the podcast.* I walked past the courtyard, pleasantly surprised to find it nearly empty. Pool's crew weren't there. They were the ones I expected to tease me about the podcast.

Raine cornered me after lunch with a dramatic, "Okay, so . . . don't freak-out."

"You can't start a conversation that way. The warning alone activates my freak-out mode," I joked. "What's going on?"

"I just got word from a source in the office that Tiffany Lancaster will be allowed to walk at graduation, but she is not actually graduating."

My hand flew to my mouth, and I spoke through my fingers. "Because of the photos?"

Raine nodded and pulled me down the hall. "They threatened expulsion, but her dad used his attorney superpower to get them to reduce it to a suspension."

"Was it us? Did we cause this?"

"Don't even go there, Storm. She did this. She posted and shared the photos."

I looked up and down the hall. "This is so not good. So not good."

"Hey, I've gotta get to class. My advice? Tell your friend to watch out."

I nodded, my mind racing. I needed to find Teresa and let her know about Tiffany's situation. But before I could even take a step toward the library, someone tapped my shoulder.

"Hey," a familiar voice said. I turned and found Pool standing there, his usually confident grin gone, replaced by tucked lips. His brows furrowed, and his eyes were dark and filled with genuine concern.

"Chantler."

"Have you heard about Tiffany?"

"No, what's going on?" I lied.

He lowered his voice. "She's in trouble."

"Seriously?" I feigned surprise.

"Yeah, it's not looking good for her." He studied me, like he was trying to read my thoughts or something.

Keep it together. Poker face! I yelled inside.

"I know there have been some issues. I mean, we've had our differences, but no one deserves to have their future ruined like that. We need to do something." As he spoke, his jaw clenched, and his hand reached up to rub his temple.

My brows shot up in confusion. "We?"

His eyes narrowed. "Teresa."

I pretended to be clueless. "Wait, I don't get it. What can she possibly do?"

"There's always a way," Pool said determinedly. "We need solid evidence—proof that Tiffany is being set up."

He stared into my eyes, and it dawned on me—Pool wanted someone else to take the fall. Conflicting emotions filled me as I absorbed his words. Part of me was happy they were finally getting what was coming to them. I guess I was experiencing a bit of epicaricacy (I had learned that word while studying for a spelling bee a few years earlier). Even though I knew Proverbs 24:17, *Rejoice not when thine enemy falleth*. Part of me was also angry at Pool's audacity, but above it all, I felt a deeper concern for Teresa's safety.

"Pool," I began cautiously, calling him by his first name and trying to keep my voice steady, "Tiffany . . . she needs to own up to her actions."

Pool's face twisted in frustration. "You don't understand. Tiffany is my girlfriend. That means I'll do whatever it takes to protect her. Teresa shouldn't have ruined everything for us."

"I don't know what you mean. Teresa is a good person. What did she do? Do you think taking down an innocent person is going to fix things? What happened to doing what's right?"

His eyes flickered with a mix of guilt and defiance. "This whole situation is messed up, all right? I just want it to be over."

Students poured into the hall from the cafeteria, heading to their next class, and several cast curious glances our way.

Pool sighed heavily, his shoulders slumping. "Tell Teresa to say it was all her. *She* had the photos taken and blamed it on Tiffany because she was jealous of her."

"I'm not getting involved. This is not my problem. I don't want anything to do with it."

"You better rethink that. You were involved enough to bring it up on that podcast. If you don't help us, then I will handle it myself."

A heavy silence hung in the air between us as Pool's words sank in. I never thought I would see this side of him—a side willing to sacrifice an innocent person for the sake of protecting his guilty girlfriend. It disgusted me.

"You know what's crazy? I wasn't even there. I don't know the details of what happened, and honestly it's really none of my business. But I do know what's right. Teresa is . . ." My chest tightened and my breaths were coming out in short gasps. "Innocent. You can't make . . . her . . . take the blame . . . just because . . . it's . . . convenient for you . . . and Tiffany." I barely got the words out, before I reached into my pocket for my inhaler.

Pool leaned forward, so close that I could smell his sweat. He grabbed my hand, preventing me from pulling my inhaler out of my pocket. My chest constricted even tighter. Panic set in as I struggled for air.

"Does this seem like a game to you, Storm?" Pool sneered, his grip on my hand tightening, like he aimed to crush it.

My eyes pleaded for him to let go, but he only seemed more amused by my discomfort. "Stop," I gasped, trying to pull away from his grasp. *I know someone sees this happening. Why aren't they helping?*

"Let go of her."

Pool released me and turned.

Raine stood there, looking like he was either going to punch or tackle him. Pool lifted his hands in surrender, trying to play it cool like we were just hanging out.

I brought the inhaler to my mouth, puffed, and inhaled.

"Man, you listened to me?" Raine shook his head. "I was hoping you wouldn't so I would have a reason to knock you the hell out."

"Maybe you'll get your chance to try," Pool replied and walked away.

Raine turned to me. "Are you okay?"

I nodded.

"Here, come with me." He led me into an empty classroom. "Sit down."

"How did you—"

"I only went to my locker. I needed to grab a book before class."

"He—"

"You don't have to say anything. I heard more than you think."

"Thank you for stepping in," I whispered, my voice quivering slightly.

Raine knelt beside my chair and grasped my hand. "No worries. I've got you."

"He totally freaked me out," I admitted.

"I know," Raine replied softly. "Pool has always been like that. He gets off on intimidating others."

I looked down at our intertwined hands, feeling grateful for his support.

"Thank you," I said again, this time with more certainty. "For having my back and standing up to him."

Raine grinned, and oh what a grin it was. "Don't worry about it. You think I'd let some creep mess with my cohost?"

Oh. I looked away. I didn't know what I expected him to say, but it wasn't that.

"Lighten up, that was a joke, Storm. I care about you."

Raine gently brushed a strand of hair behind my ear. "I like how you stood up to that jerk. You're strong, you know? No one can take that away from you." He stood. "Plus, I had to do the right thing, with the world ending and all." He winked.

My eyes widened.

"You know, the question you asked during the podcast?"

"Raine, Raine, bo-baine," Kendra sang as she bounced into the room. Have you seen—"

He pointed at me.

"Storm!" She ran over and practically flung herself onto my chair. "Did you have an attack? What the heck happened? Did you get abducted by aliens or something? You didn't come back into the cafeteria."

"I'll leave you to discuss the details," Raine said and walked out of the classroom.

"Are you okay?" asked Kendra.

I stood. For the moment, Pool, Tiffany Lancaster, and Teresa were in second place in the race for topics I wanted to discuss. "Um, I think Raine just came on to me."

Kendra's eyes widened in shock before she looked away, trying to hide a smirk.

"What? It could happen," I said, defending myself.

"I know it could. That's why I wanted you to meet him in the first place."

"But . . . ?"

"Well . . . actually, I found out he's been seeing someone."

19

— • —

Raine was a good guy who was just being friendly. I could deal with that. He's in a long-distance relationship with a girl named Nya, who lived in Atlanta. Good for him. But why was I so irritated about it? And why did he have to hold my hand? And what was with that kiss on the cheek? My other male friends didn't do any of those things.

Quit overanalyzing everything, Storm. Stop it. You're right, I replied to myself. It was time to get back down to business. I still had to complete the paper for my senior project about where I came from and how it has influenced who I am.

But just as quickly as I tried to focus, an unrelated thought popped into my head. Prom was coming up and I still didn't have a date. *Like, hello? Am I invisible or something? I could always just go solo or take Kendra, but come on, where are all the boys? If I am as hot as Kendra claimed, why aren't I getting asked out left and right? Not that I would say yes to any option that came my way.*

My scatterbrained thoughts continued to swirl as I doodled on a piece of paper in calculus class and glanced at my watch, ready to bolt out of there as soon as the bell rang. As soon as it did, I closed my notebook, exchanged a quick smile and a wave with a couple of classmates, and made a beeline for the exit. I didn't even bother going to my locker, looking for Kendra, or hitting up the vending machines.

It was one of the rare times that I was one of the first kids out of the school. I scanned the chaotic school parking lot and then the pickup line, my eyes darting from car to car, searching for Betty. But it was nowhere in sight.

Soon, a throng of students surrounded me like crows at a fast-food restaurant's dumpster—at least that's what they did in Spencer. Some hurried over to their cars. Others slumped away with overstuffed backpacks hanging from their backs, looking as if they didn't have a friend in the world, awkwardly shuffling behind groups of chattering kids.

Exhaust lingered in the air as each car in the pickup line's engine started and doors slammed shut as parents impatiently waited for the next vehicle to pull away.

I relentlessly texted my mom and even tried to call, but she didn't pick up. So I went over to a bench and pulled out my dog-eared paperback copy of *Never Really Gone* from my backpack. After getting lost in the eccentric romance of Gabby and Micah, I suddenly glanced up. I expected to see my mom's worried face staring back at me over the hood of Betty. Instead, through the chain link fence across the street, I saw that the middle school parking lot was deserted. I looked around. Only a couple of students strode away, and the cars of the pickup line were long gone.

Now I was worried. My mother never forgot about me before, like ever. Something was wrong. Before I could cue my freak-out mode, I decided to do the unthinkable—well, unthinkable to my mom—I walked.

It was so crazy that I had never walked home from school before. Our neighbors were probably going to peek through their curtains while gulping sweet tea, see me and spit the tea out on the windowpane from the shock.

I waved at the mail carrier and watched the sky through the oak trees. All the while, my freak-out mode was still engaged, not sure of what I would find when I got home. As usual, my thoughts were all over the place. What if she wasn't there at all? Maybe she was in an accident. Maybe a gator got her—my worst nightmare.

I arrived at our gravel driveway and slowed, watching my mom on the front porch. Her arms were crossed tightly over her chest like a barricade, as if trying to keep some unknown danger at bay. A tall man stood at the bottom step.

Catching sight of me, her voice was firm. "You have to go! Now!" she told him. "And don't come back!"

The man remained silent as I approached. His hand slowly lowered the bill of his worn-out hat as he took a step back. His face, hidden, held as much of a secret as mom's gun safe.

And in the hand that released his cap was a red envelope. It slipped from his grasp and landed at my feet. He left it there, climbed inside his Chevy Suburban, and drove away.

20

Every part of me tensed as I stared at the red envelope lying on the ground. I wanted to grab it, but I was so confused about what to do because I wasn't supposed to know those envelopes existed.

My mother rushed over and snatched it up before I could decide.

"Who was that man?" I asked.

She shook her head, clutching the envelope to her chest. "No one. Just a guy with the wrong address."

Lies. The red envelope she held was identical to the one in her fake gun safe. But what concerned me most was her demeanor; she seemed almost frightened. It was clear that she knew the man. "You're not acting like that was 'no one.' What's going on?" I asked. "Why are you being so weird?"

She sighed and looked away. "It's nothing for you to worry about, Storm. Just some unfinished business that's all."

I crossed my arms. "I'm not a kid anymore, Mom. You can tell me. What kind of business?"

She stared at me for a moment, her gaze heavy with unspoken words. "Okay, you're right." She sat down on the porch steps and motioned for me to join her.

I set my backpack on the ground in front of me. The rough texture of the wood pressed against my palms as I lowered onto the step, the peeling paint leaving flecks of terracotta on my palms. I brushed them off and waited for the truth behind the unwelcome visitor and the envelope.

"That man . . . he was an old friend. We lost touch years ago, after . . ." She trailed off, a faraway look in her eyes.

A moment later, she refocused on me. "I haven't heard from him since before you were born. But now, he's trying to get back in touch."

"Why?"

"I don't know. Maybe because he found out I'm single."

"Found out from whom?"

"I don't know, Storm. I'm playing a guessing game here."

I pointed at the envelope she clutched. "And what about that? Aren't you going to open it?"

She balled it up. "No, I'm not."

"But maybe it's a nice—"

"I don't care what's in it," she said and stood. Without another word, she went inside.

I sat there, staring across the street at the artificial flowers that filled Mrs. Reynold's wooden wagon flower planter beside her mailbox. Even though I didn't get a good look at the man, I would never forget his truck—especially since it showed up again a few minutes later. He pulled in front of the house, his windows tinted too dark to see inside, and paused for a moment before continuing up the road.

I watched the Suburban speed away, waiting until it had long disappeared around the corner before making my way inside. Mom sat on the sofa with one elbow resting on her knee and her hand covering her eyes.

I explained to her that I'd had an attack at school and that I spent the better part of the afternoon in the nurse's office. I left out the Pool Chantler drama.

"And they didn't call me?" she asked.

"They didn't need to."

"And you *walked* home?"

"What was I supposed to do? You forgot about me. You were too busy here with that random guy," I said and walked away. "And you know what? I enjoyed it. I like walking home. I need to do more of it."

"Storm . . ."

I went to my bedroom and closed the door. Something didn't add up about her story, but I had too much on my mind to give it more thought. All I wanted to do was blast some music and either start the day over or forget about it altogether.

My phone buzzed. "Hello?"

"Seriously, Storm? You ditched me after school?" asked Kendra.

"I bolted after calculus."

"Oh shoot, what happened?"

"Why do you ask that?"

"I can hear it in your voice."

"Just some mom-melodrama. It's nothing." I looked for my headphones, fighting with myself about whether or not to tell her about Pool. Kendra was so blinded by the fake persona he put on that she didn't see the real him.

But if I kept quiet, what if he invited her to one of his parties, and she went? I pictured it like a scene from a film: a house full of partying kids, suffocating cigarette smoke, and a sea of red plastic cups. Me, bursting in and trying to drag Kendra out, then getting shoved back outside by a bunch of wasted kids, leaving me banging on the door like a crazy person, desperately trying to save her.

"Storm? Earth to Storm. Ground control to Storm."

"Oh, sorry. I was lost in thought."

"Evidently." Her tone turned serious. "Okay, for real though. Tell me what's going on."

Because of my daydream, I told Kendra exactly what happened at school.

"I'm kicking his gorgeous butt. Do you hear me? I'm kicking his High School Musical-looking, Mean Girls-movie-watching, corn chip-breath-smelling, jeans too tight in the thighs-wearing butt."

I couldn't contain my laughter. Even though I knew she was serious, I couldn't help it. "Calm down," I said, still cracking up. "It's not me I'm worried about."

"Wait, wait, wait," Kendra said in her signature exaggerated way. She does that when something is really weird or off-the-charts crazy. "It's about to get real."

"It already is."

"Well, both Tiffany and Teresa were no-shows today. Maybe neither are coming back."

"I don't know, but right now, I've got my own problems."

"You mean Raine?"

"No, I don't mean Raine. Why would he be a problem?"

"Because you low-key like him, and you're upset that he has a girlfriend."

I sat at the end of my bed and kicked off my Jordans. "I just think he's cool, and I like him as a friend, okay? Don't get it twisted."

"Awww, it's adorbs when you try to use slang. Weird, but adorbs. All right, I gotta hit the books before Bible study. You coming?"

I looked out my window at the church parking lot. "Yeah, I'll see you there. Bye."

21

I flopped back on my bed and stared up at the ceiling. Did I really like Raine as more than a friend? I barely knew him, but there was something about him that made me feel . . . different. A good kind of different.

What was wrong with me? I had just gone through the whole, "I think it's Todd and he likes me." Now, I was having feelings for Raine?

Kendra said I wasn't boy crazy like the rest of the girls. I think she jinxed me. Better late than never, I guess.

With a sigh, I hauled myself off my bed to get some work done before Bible study.

Two hours, a stack of completed homework, and a bowl of ramen later, I yelled up the stairs from the living room, "Mom! Are you going to church?"

"You go ahead, I think I'm going to lay down for a bit."

"Okay. I'm going through the back."

"Be careful!"

Our backyard was the gateway to heaven. Well, not literally. On the other side of the fence was the back of the church's sprawling property. Our house had belonged to the former presiding pastor, but the church sold it when he retired. After Mom bought it, she kept the gate that led from our yard to the church's property. "This way we'll never be late to service!" she'd said.

I carefully stepped through the weeds near the fence—it was my worst nightmare to come across a snake—and pushed open the gate. On the church side, the lawn was perfectly manicured. Someone really needed to bring a weed trimmer to our side.

The parking lot was already packed. I scanned the crowd, looking for familiar faces. A few members of the congregation waved or nodded as I walked by. But my usual group of friends were nowhere to be seen.

Finally, I spotted Kendra kneeling in front of a stroller, talking in a sing-song way to Mrs. Hanson's baby.

I positioned myself where she could see me, but I didn't go near them. I wasn't in the mood to be my I-love-everybody self.

Kendra wiggled a finger in little DJ's face and glanced in my direction. "Storm!" she exclaimed and waved like she doesn't see me every single day.

"Hey!" I replied, trying to plaster a smile on my face.

She walked over with a brow raised. "Great. You're doing that thing you do with your face. Everything is not okay, is it?"

"No, I'm just tired, I guess," I replied with a shrug, hoping Kendra wouldn't pry further. I didn't want to dump my drama on her. Now wasn't the time.

As we strolled into the church together, heading straight for the youth department, my mind continued to do its own little dance, despite my best efforts to focus. All the other teens were engaged in the youth pastor's message on trusting God in uncertain times, but as I flipped through my Bible, my thoughts bounced from Raine, to the mysterious man with the red envelope, to my mom and the gun safe, to Teresa and the school drama, and finally to the apocalyptic dream that continued to tug at me like a persistent toddler.

The double doors behind me swung open, and I caught a glimpse of a few latecomers. A tall figure walked in behind them. He kept his head low and quickly made his way to an empty seat in the back row.

I spun forward. *It's him. Is he following me? My mother is alone. Now would be the time for him to talk to her, but he's here?*

I tried not to be obvious, using my shoulder to scratch the side of my face, and strained to get a better look at his face. He was too far away.

A gentle nudge from Kendra brought my attention back to Pastor Rodney. "What's up?" she whispered.

I shook my head and tried, again, to pay attention, but it was no use. A feeling of unease settled in my stomach.

As soon as the service ended, I craned my neck, trying to spot the man. But he was gone. Just like that, he had slipped out unnoticed. I shook my head. *It probably wasn't even him.*

Of course it was, I argued back at myself.

Kendra hooked her arm through mine, guiding me from the row of chairs and out into the bustling lobby. I pulled away and hurried outside, scanning the parking lot. I was determined to confront the guy someplace where I felt safe and surrounded by saints. I was confident I was going to get the answers my mother wouldn't give me.

But there was no sign of him.

"What is it? Did you see Teresa? Was she here?" Kendra asked, catching up to me.

"No. I thought I did."

Total lie. Right there on holy grounds. *Forgive me, God.*

22

— · —

I stood at the fence and stared at the back of my house. The windows were dark, not a single light shining from inside. A car backing up in the church parking lot broke through the stillness, its headlights briefly illuminating my path to the back door.

Something was up. My mother never turned off all the lights this early. I practically sprinted through the backyard while I could still see where I was going. Thankfully, the flood light flashed on, and I hurried inside.

Even in the dark, I knew where everything was in my house. I set my purse on the table and walked across the kitchen. I guess my mom wasn't joking when she said she was going to lie down.

I opened the refrigerator to grab some juice, twisted off the cap, and took a big swallow.

"Storm . . ."

I gulped and set the bottle down. *Why is she sitting in the dark?* I switched on the light above the sink. My mother sat in a chair, leaning against the wall. *Sheesh, what happened. I've only been gone an hour and a half.*

"You think you know men, but you don't." Her voice held a drawl I wasn't accustomed to hearing from her, nor the slur. I charged over and grabbed the bottle of liquor out of her hands.

She reached for the bottle. "What are you doing?"

"You're on medication, you can't have this!"

"I'm the mother. I decide—" Her hands dropped, and her words lowered to an indistinguishable mumble as I poured what was left of the bottle down the drain. I hadn't seen this side of her in a few years.

"Stormie . . ."

"Let me take you up to bed."

"You're so good to me. I haven't been good to you," she said as she tried to stand. I caught her around the waist, and she put an arm around my neck.

"I took your life from you."

"No, you didn't, Mom. I still have it." I would've taken her to brush her teeth if I thought it would help with the smell.

Tears streamed down her face. "You don't know boys. What you see here in Spencer is not all there is. And then, you meet one who is different than anyone you have ever met, one who sweeps you away when you least expect it. Someone you never thought you would fall in love with, and then . . ."

I decided against the stairs and led her to the sofa. She plopped down hard, going straight from standing to lying.

"But you love me, right?"

"Mom, you know I do."

"Then you forgive me?"

"For what? Mom, please rest. Just go to sleep. We'll talk more in the morning."

She only stared at me as I pulled a throw blanket from the back of the sofa and laid it over her. In minutes, she was asleep, her chest steadily rising and falling. I watched her for a while and smoothed her hair back from her face.

As I turned away to walk upstairs, I realized that for my mother to start drinking again meant the man—whoever he was—was more important than I'd thought.

First thing the next morning, I went downstairs to check on her. Normally, she would be making sure I was up or that I had my inhaler and was not on the verge of an attack. Now, the roles had reversed; it was my turn to tend to her and make sure she was okay.

There were still a couple of hours before sunlight would spill through the windows, so it was still dark in the house. I half expected my mom to still be asleep, but when I entered the living room, she wasn't there. The throw was folded and placed neatly on the arm of the sofa, and clanking noises came from the kitchen.

"Mom?" I walked to the back of the house. She had showered and dressed in scrubs for work. "What are you doing?" I asked, relieved that she was up and seemingly back to her normal self.

She held up a mug with a smile. "You know the routine. Chamomile tea. Want some?"

"Umm . . . sure," I said hesitantly as I sat down at the kitchen table. Just last night she'd sat in the same seat, drunk and barely able to walk, and now it was like it never happened.

She set a mug in front of me. Had she really forgotten everything that happened? Or was she just pretending?

"So . . . what happened last night?" I asked cautiously as she sat beside me.

"What do you mean?"

There was no easy way to say it. "You were drunk. I tossed your bottle of liquor."

Her face fell for a moment before she quickly regained her composure.

"Oh . . . that," she said dismissively. "I just had a rough day yesterday."

"Just a rough day?" I asked incredulously. "Mom, you haven't touched alcohol in years."

"I know, Storm," she said with a sigh. Silence hung between us for a moment before she spoke again, slowly, as if carefully choosing her words. "Stormie, can we just forget about last night? It was a mistake, and it won't happen again. I promise."

I hesitated before nodding, while dabbing at my tea bag with a spoon. *I'm so tired of the secrets.*

23

— • —

The rest of the morning was like a replay of most mornings: Kendra texting *#OOTD* with photos, me responding with pictures of my own outfit of the day, and Mom dropping me off at school on her way to work.

As we pulled in front of Beacon High, anxiety churned in my gut at the thought of facing Pool. I reached for the door handle, and my mom's hand covered my free hand, offering a gentle squeeze before I got out of Betty.

"I love you, Stormie. I always want what's best for you, even though I know I make mistakes," she said in a gentle tone.

I felt a twinge of guilt even though I didn't do anything wrong. I didn't even judge her. Meeting her eyes, I managed a small smile and replied, "I know, Mom. I love you too."

She watched me walk away and pulled out of the drop-off line with a wave. "Have a great day!" she yelled as she drove off.

"Sure thing, Mom," I muttered to myself and walked inside the school.

The Beacon High hallways buzzed with an undercurrent of excitement. Lockers slammed in rhythm to hushed whispers and stifled laughter at a secret shared among everyone but me. I was usually the last to know anything, so no surprise there.

Amidst the chatter, I found a huddle of familiar faces—all wearing different dark blue or black hoodies, their eyes wide, heads bent over a cell phone screen.

My first thought was, *Oh no. Another Teresa pic has surfaced.* But their hushed tones revealed a different name, one that made me perk up with interest. Their whispers were like music to my ears. And then came the words: "hot dog farm."

My breath caught in my throat. Real friends will do the craziest things for you. I just had to figure out which friend it was.

"I heard Pool went ballistic," said the boy holding the phone.

Another boy nodded. "Whoever did this is a legend."

"I wouldn't go that far. But you know what? You reap what you sow."

"Yeah, sounds like karma finally caught up with him."

A smile spread across my face as Pool's public humiliation became the talk of the day—and not a single mention of Teresa or the embarrassing photos.

Rumor had it there were a bunch of "Hot Dog Farm" signs that led up to a house, and one of our classmates followed it—perhaps many of them. They probably thought the signs would lead them to a Dachshund breeder.

Instead, on Pool's lawn were about a hundred hot dogs skewered and planted firmly in the ground.

How they did it, or how many of them it took to do it, I had no idea. But it was what Pool's family awoke to that morning, and from what I heard, their camera only picked up a shadowy figure spraying some kind of foam over the lens on their doorbell. I don't know how much truth there was to the foam bit. It sounded like someone made it up to add to the story.

If only Pool didn't live on the opposite end of town. I would've loved to have seen a hot dog lawn in such an affluent neighborhood, with their stone roads and professionally manicured lawns. The idea was genius; Pool was a "dog" if I ever saw one.

At lunch, I spotted Raine across the cafeteria, standing out like a neon sign in a city of white lights, his curly hair just as big and wild as usual. He caught my eye and, with a flick of his wrist, gestured me over. The taste of steamed vegetables lingered in my mouth as I walked toward him. I sucked at my teeth, hoping I didn't have carrots stuck between them. The mischievous glint in his eyes, practically screamed, "It was me!"

"Hey," he said with a grin. "Enjoying today's gossip?"

I laughed. "You did it, didn't you? The hot dog farm on Pool's lawn?"

He held his hands up. "Unfortunately, I can't take credit for it. But I have mad respect for whoever pulled that off. See you Saturday." Raine sauntered off with the casual, unbothered manner I'd become accustomed to, and although he denied involvement, his wink spoke volumes.

Saturday loomed ahead like an adventure waiting to unfold. Little did I know, that was just the warm-up act before things got totally crazy. Like the opening act of a play before the plot twists and turns like a rollercoaster ride through a whirlwind.

"What are you doing?" Kendra whispered in my ear and giggled.

"Nothing." I sped away, realizing I had been standing there watching Raine—in front of the cafeteria staff, some juniors, and most of the senior class.

On Saturday morning, I hurried to the front door. "Mom, I'm gone!"

"Where to?"

"I already told you, to the school with Kendra. Her dad is dropping us off." I still hadn't told her about the podcast.

"Where's my kiss?"

"We're late!" I groaned and ran back to the kitchen, kissed her, and shot out the door.

Raine had texted me the night before, asking me to invite Kendra to be a guest on the show to add some variety. She was more than happy to oblige.

I hopped in the back seat of Mr. J's truck. "Hey, girl," said Kendra.

"Hey, Storm," said her dad.

"Thanks for dropping us off." I glanced at my phone and read the text from Raine: *Where are you?*

"No problem," said Mr. J. "I'm just happy that your productivity is rubbing off on this one," he said, motioning his head toward Kendra.

I grinned, wondering what exactly she had told her father we would be doing. A few minutes later, we hopped out of the truck and hurried over to the side entrance of the school where Rick Young, Raine's assistant, saw us from the window and let us in. I couldn't understand how he managed to see anything with his bangs sweeping down to his chin.

We power walked down the empty school corridor. The only noise, aside from the rhythmic tapping of our shoes against the floor, was the faint music drifting out of the open door of the band room.

I figured Beacon High was serious about keeping their electric bill down because the school was pretty dark. Only a few lights flicked on in the library as we entered and went to the back room.

Rick held the door open, and I rushed in and mouthed "sorry" to Raine. He pointed at the mic beside his and I scuttered over.

"I'm the bad boy, Raine . . ."

I cut him off. "And I'm the good girl, Storm."

His brows raised in surprise, and he grinned. "We're unlikely friends bringing you this week's podcast episode. Welcome to Things We Don't Tell Our Parents: Uncensored, streaming on SpotOver and FICast, where we discuss how to survive high school. It's about to go down: From the drama and the homework, to the friends and the enemies, and all the hilarious moments in between—we've got you covered.

"So listen, contrary to most of the kids at our school, I like high school," said Raine.

"Me too," I replied. "Especially when the craziest things happen."

"I know where you're going with this. The hot dog farm, right?"

I nodded. "Yes."

"If you don't attend Beacon High, then maybe you're not aware of what happened this week. If you do attend and you still don't know, we're going to need to get you some friends." Raine went on to tell them about the hot dogs. He finished by adding, "Now we're not saying whose lawn it was, but I hear the student's parents are on the warpath, threatening lawsuits and expulsion."

"It was only a prank, though. And no one knows who did it."

"Yeah, that's life. One prank after another. By the way, Storm, you're looking rather cute today."

"Am I? That was random." I suddenly felt like a radio co-host.

"Wait, are those pajama bottoms? Rick, don't you hate when girls do that?"

"Yeah, and crocs," he shouted.

"Which I'm wearing also," I replied.

"Oops."

"You're not insulting me. I'm comfortable."

Raine laughed. "Did you have any quintessential problems this week like the rest of us at school?"

I thought about how to bring up the issue with Pool. But I decided I didn't want to.

"Say something," he mouthed, snapping me out of my thoughts.

"Uh . . . My senior project sucks."

"Do tell."

"I have to write about my family history, which I don't know anything about."

"Can't you ask your mother?"

"There's no one but us."

"That's tough. At least you don't have to deal with your aunt's disgusting fruit cake or boring family parties where they expect you to just sit there and listen when you could be in your bedroom or out doing other things."

"I don't know what that's like. So for me, it might be a good issue to have," I replied.

"True. But the question is, how do we solve this problem, people?"

The listeners added their suggestions to the chat on the social media live feed.

"Jessica says 'make up something.' Dishonest much, Jessica? Hmm . . . Kelly says she wishes she didn't have family. Not cool, Kelly."

"You said, 'she'," I pointed out. "Kelly could be a male, you know?"

"Yeah, you're right. My bad, Kels. Oh, here's a good one. Joshua says 'swab your mouth and do one of those DNA tests. You'll find out where you're from.' What do you think?"

"I couldn't do that."

"Yeah, you could. Joshua saved the day."

I jumped in my seat as Rick rang a bell to celebrate Joshua.

"You can let us know the results right here on the podcast," said Raine. He squinted at me as if peering deep inside my genetic makeup. "I'm thinking Portugal, with some Scotland and Wales."

"Whatever. Anyway, I don't have that kind of money."

"It's not expensive. I know you've been saving for college. Isn't it worth it to dip into that? You have to finish your senior project, don't you? And I know you want an A."

"Right . . . Okay, I'll do it."

Raine typed on his phone. "There. I just sent you the link. Do it now."

"I don't have anything with me."

He dug into his pocket and pulled out his wallet. "Here, put it on my card."

I glanced at Kendra. She nodded, seemingly excited.

"You have to promise to open the results here. Oh, wait a minute." Raine read a comment. "Mel says, 'My mom has done it, and they will email you the results.' That works. You can pull it up here, live on the show."

I shrugged. "Okay."

"See how we did that, solving problems in real time? I love us," said Raine.

Rick and Raine shared a moment of camaraderie, and I caught Kendra's amused expression. She watched me watching Raine, knowing I was crushing hard.

24

Under the bright studio lights, as the scent of brewed coffee and cream wafted from Raine's cafe cup, Raine and I huddled together, our heads bowed in quiet consultation. We poured over our list of potential questions for Kendra before the next episode, so she would have time to think about them before we got started.

Raine introduced the podcast and gave a brief introduction of our guest before jumping into the conversation. "You all know her. The girl with the long braids."

"Boho braids," Kendra shouted.

"All right. Boho braids it is." He said the next part in Spanish, and I was thoroughly impressed. "You don't have to know what I said, but she does because she's also bilingual. She's like a sister to everyone she loves, but a deadly viper to those she can't stand . . ."

Oddly enough, his description was pretty accurate. Kendra gave a nod for each description and a fist in the air for the last.

She was totally at ease at the mic, answering Raine's questions with confidence and the humor we needed for an epic episode. When it was my turn to ask a question, I went with my go-to query. "What if you knew the date the world would end? What would you do differently?"

Kendra paused before answering. "Honestly, I wouldn't change a thing. Knowing when it's all going to end would just make me appreciate every moment even more."

"I like that," said Raine, nodding his head in approval.

"It's true though," Kendra continued. "I've learned from losing my stepmom in a car accident that life is precious and that we should make the most of it while we can. It's a balance . . . I may not be afraid to go off on someone when I'm upset, but I'm just as quick to forgive, have grace, or be kind. People at school may think I'm over the top or whatever, but at least I'm honest and living as best as any girl my age can."

Raine pointed at her. "That's why we vibe." Then, he went off in a whole other direction. "Braid my hair for me."

"Random much?" I asked as I laughed.

"Raine, you have a lot of hair," said Kendra.

"Seriously, who's French braiding all the boys' hair at school? Somebody put the deets in the chat. Hook a brother up."

"Good show," Raine told us after we wrapped. "I mean shows. And thanks for agreeing to do the DNA test, Storm."

"Thanks for paying for it."

"Of course, anything for the content!"

"Oh, was that all it was?" I replied with an eyeroll. "That's exactly what's wrong with the world today, 'anything for content.' Whatever." I tugged at the hair hanging in his face. "I'll give it a shot."

Raine looked confused. "What are you talking about?"

I moved behind his chair. "Your hair." His long wild curls fell in every direction.

"Are you saying you can braid?" He turned to look up at me in disbelief.

"Why wouldn't I be able to?" I asked, slightly offended. "Because I'm white? Kendra, give me a comb."

"I have braids. Why would I carry a comb? Plus I wouldn't want his cooties on my comb. I have a brush for my edges . . ."

"I have a pick," said Raine. "Here, I have to see this."

"That'll work. Give it here." His hair was surprisingly soft and a little oily from whatever he used on it. I parted off a section near the top and slowly started braiding from his hairline back.

"Ouch, girl! Don't rip my follicles out," Raine joked, wincing slightly.

"Beauty is pain," I teased.

Kendra filmed the whole thing, and while it wasn't my best braiding, I managed a nice cornrow. "There. Check it out," I told him.

Raine pressed his fingers along his braid. "Woah, I'm impressed." He stood. "I've gotta go, but you owe me a full head."

I laughed at him. "Do not walk out of here with a braid down the center of your head."

"Why not? Be proud of your work, Storm. I am."

"No, seriously. You look crazy."

"I can't take it," Kendra said as she pushed him back down into a chair and reached for his braid. He tried to stand up, so I sat on his lap.

"Rick, are you just going to let them double-team me like this?"

"Dude, they're right. That hair will ruin your rep."

"Done," said Kendra after she'd unraveled the braid, and I stood to leave.

"Bye ladies. The time we have together is always fun."

"You're so weird," Kendra replied as we walked away.

I stopped walking and turned back. "Wait. Admit it."

Raine eyes swept left and right. "I don't know what you're talking about. Oh, the hot dog farm? Listen, hypothetically, if I *did* plant those hot dogs, you know Pool had it coming."

I nodded and winked. "Hypothetically."

"It wasn't me."

"We believe you," Kendra said and pulled me outside and through the library.

"I still don't believe him."

"Who cares about that? Really, Storm, how did I do?

I looked into her eyes, seeing how serious she was about it. "You were so good. I was blown away. How did you do that?"

She shrugged. "I just tried to be real, you know?"

"No, I mean it," I insisted. "The way you talked about your stepmom . . . it got me thinking about my own life. I don't want to wake up one day full of regret, wishing I'd done more with the time I had."

Kendra nodded. "Yeah, well, you're the one who put all of these mature thoughts in my mind. "We just never know how long we've get. Gotta make the most of it."

25

A week had passed since I saw that creepy guy at my doorstep and at church, and I still couldn't shake the unease. It was giving me the heebie-jeebies. Every time I thought of him and that bright red envelope, my mind went into overdrive trying to come up with conspiracy theories. *Was he a secret agent? Was he just some weirdo obsessed with my mom? What was it about him that drove her to drink?*

My mother, who usually shared everything with me, refused to talk about what happened or even acknowledge his existence, pretending it never happened.

But I couldn't forget about it. Every time I saw a pickup truck on the road, my heart raced and my palms got clammy, and the thoughts would start again: *Was it him? Is he watching us?*

I tried to tell myself that I was overreacting, but something in my gut told me otherwise. Why didn't he say anything when he saw me? Instead, he'd dropped the envelope. He wanted me to see it and pick it up.

He wants me to know.

"Hey, what's going on with you?" Kendra asked. "And don't say 'nothing,' because you've been different for a couple of weeks. And just now, you didn't even notice I was talking to you until I nudged you."

We walked outside the school and sat on a bench. I debated whether or not to tell her what was happening, but before I could make a decision, Todd came up behind us on his skateboard.

"Ladies," he said with a grin.

"Can you give me a ride home on that?" asked Kendra.

"You've always got jokes. What's up, Storm? You look like you've got something on your mind."

Until he mentioned it, I hadn't realized I was frowning. "Yeah, no. Senior project, you know. This grade will make or break me." I replied vaguely.

Todd smirked. "Not you. You're the smartest person I know. I mean, not that I know you. I mean, not like that."

Kendra lifted a brow at him.

He cleared his throat. "So, did you find out who sent the text?"

"Yeah," was all I said.

"Okay then," Todd replied and looked away like someone was calling him. "I'll catch up with you later." He kicked off and rolled away on his skateboard.

"Okay, Storm, spill," Kendra demanded. "What's really going on with you? *Maze Runner* boy was trying to— Never mind. There's your car."

We dropped Kendra off, then Mom dropped me off. She said she had errands to run.

I went inside the house and stood with my back against the front door, my eyes glued to the stairs. *This is your chance*, I told myself and hurried up to my mother's closet.

The gun safe was in its usual spot, and I took it down. There was a new envelope on top of the pile. My heart raced as I carefully opened it, making sure I didn't leave behind any trace of my snooping.

Inside *this* red envelope was a handwritten letter and a small key.

Dearest Rebecca,

I hope this letter finds you well. It's been too long since we've seen each other, and I am plagued with years of regret over what I did to you. I pray that after sixteen years, you can find forgiveness in your heart.

I've searched for you for a long time. Please believe I wish you no ill will. Enclosed is a key to a safety deposit box at First National Bank on Main Street. Leave it inside. Please. It will change everything.

Meet me there at 4 pm, any day. I will not stop waiting for your return.

Sincerely,

Clarence

This guy knew my mother's name and where she lived. And he seemed desperate to see her again. I tried to recall if she had ever mentioned someone named Clarence. Sure, she'd had a life before she popped me out of her womb, but until recently, it wasn't something I thought much about. She was just my cool, child-obsessed mother who hovered and worried too much and allowed me to skip school once in a while for movie streaming and chill days.

After returning the envelope to the safe, I compared the return addresses on the other envelopes. They all had the same address scribbled across the top left corner.

But why the secrets and the lies? They threatened to spiral out of control until they became a whirlwind, tearing apart every sane thing they came in contact with.

At least, that's what was beginning to happen at my house. My mom had too many secrets. I often watched her, wondering, *How can you sit there like you're so holy when you're hiding things and lying to your daughter?*

Confronting her was not an option. She could be fragile, and I didn't want her falling into one of her bouts of depression. She hardly needed to see her therapist now.

The following day, my mom picked me up from school and uttered my favorite words. "Ramen?"

"Yes, absolutely. Of course. Why are we still here? What took you so long to ask?"

"All of that, huh?"

I nodded.

"What? No lunch today?"

"Hardly. Mom, I think I should've been homeschooled."

"Well, you were until middle school."

"I don't think we should've stopped. It's a hard world out here."

"And you're just now realizing that in your senior year, after begging to go to school with Kendra?"

"At the time, I didn't understand the dynamics of it all."

"Well you only have about a month left to go, so suck it up, girlie. You asked for it, you got it. Make the moments count, you know. You'll never experience your high school days again."

"Yeah, that's true."

My mom pulled Betty into a parking space in front of the post office. I picked up the key from the center console. "I'll get the mail. You get the ramen, because I know how much it means to you to treat your beautiful, amazing daughter to her favorite food."

"All right. I'll meet you back here, but remember, Betty is the black car with the pollen-covered hood. Got it?"

I saluted her and walked over to the door with the American flag on it. There were a few people in line in the small space crowded with greeting cards, shipping boxes, and stationery supplies. I walked around them to the P.O. boxes, past number 1452, and backed up when I spotted it. Just as I was about to insert the key into the box, a voice startled me, making me jump and drop the key.

"I didn't mean to scare you, girlie."

That's weird, my mom just called me that too. I recognized him, but this was the first time I saw his face close up. "Why-why are you following me?" I demanded. "And what's up with those red envelopes?"

The man stared at me for a moment before breaking into an eerie grin. "You're one of the chosen ones," he said in a low, guttural voice. "The message will reveal your destiny."

I gasped.

He broke into the most awful snorting fit of laughter that made everyone waiting in line at the counter glance over. "It was a joke. I got that from a book."

I glared at him. "Who are you?"

"A name that would mean nothing to you."

"Were you waiting for my mother?"

"Your mother needs to face her past. Do you even know who your father is?"

"Of course I do. He died."

"Yeah, he died," he said slowly.

I turned the key, opened the box, and retrieved the mail, thinking he would leave, but he didn't. Hopefully, the post office would remain busy in case I needed witnesses.

"Well, I have to go." I turned to walk past him but stopped. "Is there something you want me to tell my mother?"

"Nope."

"Then stop bothering us." I started to walk away, then stopped again. "There is no First National Bank on Main Street. I checked."

His eyes widened, as if realizing I knew more than he thought. "It's not in Spencer."

"Where is it?"

"Ask your mother," he replied.

This time, *he* walked away, the heels of his cowboy boots clicking across the floor. He didn't look back, totally confident with whatever he was keeping from me. Maybe he thought I would follow him. Not. I could just hear the customers. "Yeah, we saw a girl who fits that description, Officer. She followed some guy out of the post office and then disappeared. Oh, you found her body in a ditch, two towns west? I'm not surprised."

I shook my head, trying to banish the crazy thoughts swirling around. I had a firm belief in thinking something into existence, and this was something I definitely didn't want to come true.

I left the post office, went next door, and gave Bryson a little wave as I entered the shop. He shot me a huge happy grin and pointed me towards my mom, who was sitting at our usual spot, where we liked to people-watch and create ridiculous scenarios about their conversations. Giving Bryson a thumbs up, I slid into the seat across from my mom.

"Here ya go," I said, handing her the mail. "Unfortunately, there was nothing for me." I ignored the red envelope in the short stack as if it were just a piece of junk mail.

Mom slipped the stack into her oversized purse on the chair beside her and glanced over at Bryson with a weird grin.

Oh no, here it comes. "Mom, please."

"Please what? I didn't do anything."

"Yet. I see it coming. Do not tell him to ask me to the prom."

"Who, me?" She innocently batted her eyelashes.

"Mom . . ."

"Okay, okay. I'll play nice for now."

26

L aughter and jeers echoed off the white cinder block walls of Beacon High. Amongst it all, a lone figure stood out like a flamingo in a flock of vultures—Raine. His eyes searched the crowd until they locked on me, and he grinned. He might as well have blown me a kiss, the way my heart fluttered.

But tension thickened in the air as his gaze shifted, locking on Pool across the courtyard.

A month had passed and Raine still checked on me every day—a guardian angel with a devil-may-care attitude. He was one of the few who wasn't afraid of Pool. But for some reason, Pool seemed afraid of *him*. Raine was too unpredictable, I suppose. A wild card. They didn't know how far he would go or what he might do.

"Who's doing this?" Pool screamed as he stormed through the front doors of the school the next day. I watched from a distance as he shoved a timid freshman out of his way, knocking him over a trash can. Pool's fists clenched as he scanned the hallway.

Right, because yelling at a bunch of students always results in a confession. Like someone would really raise a hand and say, "It was me, Pool. I'm the mastermind behind the pranks." Not.

This time, I heard that Pool found his yard covered in a million—okay, maybe just a few hundred—white plastic forks. But being "forked" was not what got him so riled up.

After his family supposedly hired extra security, someone was able to use some kind of weed killer and doused his lawn. Most of the grass was lush and green, but where the grass was dead was the word "BULLY" spelled out in large letters, facing the street so that anyone who drove by could read it clearly.

Suddenly, a crumpled ball of paper flew through the air and bounced off Pool's head. He whipped around to see where it came from. On the other side of the hall, Raine leaned casually against the wall, twirling a pen between his fingers. He met Pool's stare and gave him a sly wink.

"You think you're funny, don't you, Thunder?" Pool said as he approached Raine.

"Ha!" said Raine. "You called me 'Thunder.' That's—that's actually pretty cool. But I have no idea what you're talking about."

Pool jabbed a finger towards Raine's face. "I know it was you who messed up my lawn."

Raine didn't flinch. He kept his hazel eyes locked on Pool's. "Prove it," he said simply.

Pool's face turned red. He knew he didn't have any actual evidence. "I'm gonna get you for this," he said through gritted teeth.

Raine leaned in close and said in a low voice, "I look forward to it."

The two boys stared each other down for a long tense moment before the security officers headed up the hall. Pool turned and stormed away, and I let out a breath I didn't realize I'd been holding, watching the whole thing go down. Raine caught my eye and gave me a subtle wink before sauntering off down the hall.

But Raine's protection was limited to the school. I wish he had been around later that day, when I went swimming without my mom.

She had dropped me off and agreed I could walk home. Alone. I couldn't believe that was something we even had to argue about.

I walked into the center, scanned my ID, said my hellos to Mrs. Tracey, then went to the locker room and changed into my bathing suit. As soon as I lowered into the swimming pool, I took a deep breath and dove into the water, my body slicing through the surface and leaving a trail of bubbles in my wake. When I resurfaced at the far end, I turned and swam back to the other side. This time, I stopped, lifted my goggles, and looked around.

"What are you doing here?" I asked the man stooping at the edge of the pool. I looked over my shoulder. Mrs. Tracey wasn't there. She never left her post.

"You don't remember me, do you?" he asked.

"You already know I don't know who you are," I replied and looked over at the other swimmers.

"Yeah, you do," he replied through the toothpick he chewed on. "Think harder."

He walked away, and I stayed right there, frozen in that spot, until he was gone. Why was he showing up wherever I was? *I thought it was my mom he wanted to talk to.*

I leaned back against the pool wall. There was something vaguely familiar about his face, and as I walked home, I suddenly remembered what he smelled like from up close.

He carried me. Wait . . . I had an attack and he . . . He carried me?

I raced home as fast as I could, sprinted up the front steps, and threw open the front door. "Mom!" I shouted as I hurried through the house. I continued to shout her name until I found her upstairs.

"Storm, what's wrong? Calm down. Breathe."

"I just remembered something."

"Okay," she said slowly, holding the dust rag and spray bottle midair.

"That man who was here when I walked home that day, I've seen him before. It's been years, but I remember his face."

"That's impossible," she replied and turned away.

"Impossible that I remember him, or impossible that I've seen him before? Mom, stop dusting. Who is he?"

She gave one last swipe over her dresser but didn't face me. "No one."

"You're lying," I said.

"Storm!" She placed the hand holding the dust cloth on her hip. "I didn't raise you to talk to me like that."

"You're lying, and I'm tired of it," I told her, then rushed to my bedroom and slammed the door.

For once, she didn't call after me or check on me, and I guess neither of us wanted dinner. She left me to my thoughts for the rest of the night, which I was grateful for. The silence worked for me. If she wasn't going to tell me the truth, then I wasn't interested in hearing what she had to say.

The house remained dark and quiet. The later it became, the more I worried about my mother's PTSD and feared she might have more liquor hidden somewhere in the house. So in the middle of the night, I crept down the hallway and gently pushed open her bedroom door.

She was sound asleep.

"Mom," I started. "I'm sorry—" She usually woke easily, but she didn't even stir. "Mom?" I shook her, but she didn't wake. "Mom!" I screamed, then noticed a bottle of sleeping pills open on her nightstand.

I picked up the bottle. It was empty.

"No, no, no, no! You can't do this to me. Wake up!" I shook her harder, tears streaming down my face. "Mom, please wake up!" I begged.

But she remained still, her breathing slow and shallow.

I ran to the phone and, with trembling fingers, dialed 911. "M-my mom, she took a bunch of pills," I cried into the phone. "Please send help!"

"What is your name?" asked the operator.

"My name?" For a second, I couldn't remember. "My name is Storm. Storm Davis."

"And what is your address?"

"I don't know. Can't you trace the call? Send someone to help us."

"I need you to stay calm, Storm. Take a deep breath."

I inhaled deeply, exhaled, and told her our address.

"Good job, Storm. Is your mother breathing?"

"Yes, yes she is."

"That's good. We have an ambulance on the way."

She stayed on the phone with me until the ambulance arrived a few minutes later. I opened the front door, and the paramedics charged up the stairs to where she lay unconscious. They loaded her onto a stretcher, and I sank to the floor, hugging my knees to my chest.

"Are you coming with us?"

"Yes," I replied and hopped up, then grabbed my mother's handbag and ran to get mine.

At the hospital, I paced the waiting room while doctors worked to stabilize my mom. I was freezing, wearing only a T-shirt and pajama pants, so a kind nurse brought me a blanket and a cup of tea, but I couldn't drink it. All I could do was pray for my mom.

After what felt like an eternity, a doctor came out to speak with me. "Your mother is stable," he said gently. "We were able to pump her stomach and counteract the effects of the overdose."

"Can I see her?"

"Follow me."

I let out a shaky breath, flooded with relief as I saw her resting peacefully in the hospital bed. I knew when she woke we would have a long road ahead. I had no idea her depression had gotten so bad. I should have paid closer attention, been kinder.

But I wouldn't make that mistake again. From then on, I'd be right by her side, giving her the strength she needed—no matter which stranger showed up from her past.

We stood in the doorway, and the doctor asked, "Do you have any family that can come and get you?"

27

—·—

Although I was a senior in high school, I was a year younger than the rest of my classmates and still a minor.

Kendra's father had been the emergency contact on all my school paperwork since my freshman year, so I gave his information to the hospital administrator.

Mr. J and Kendra picked me up, and I stayed with them, sharing Kendra's haven of flowers. They hung from her bedroom ceiling by thin wires, creating the illusion of flowers floating in the air all around us.

The Medinas endured my sulking and not eating with concerned glances. But after a week of it, Kendra had had enough.

"Storm, we need to get you out of the house. You're moping around, and granted you've had reason to, but your mom is fine now, and I need to see you smile again," she said as she rebraided one of her braids that had come loose.

"It's my fault, though. If I hadn't yelled at her, she wouldn't be in this position."

"And still, you won't tell me why you went off like that. Was it that bad? I mean, you're not a mean person. How bad could it have been?" She studied my eyes, as if she had a superpower where she could look deep enough and see what I had done.

I looked away. "Where are we going?"

Kendra gave a relieved yelp. I was just glad to put an end to her questions.

"Here, put this on," she replied, tossing me a purple hoodie. "Now, let's see what we're going to do with your hair."

"Nope. You're not changing my ponytail. Be glad I'm even leaving the house."

"Fine. I won't push it, but you are in need of mascara."

She handed the wand to me, and I tossed it in the trash can.

"Seriously, Storm?" Kendra shrieked as she dug it out.

I dressed in the skinny jeans and hoodie she insisted on, and her father dropped us off at Spencer's annual festival. Usually, you could catch a livestock or horse show there, but this was the week of the carnival. There were more rides this year than I had ever seen, as well as games and food vendors, but I didn't feel like indulging. I stood in the fairgrounds parking lot feeling out of place and anxious.

"Storm, my dad texted asking if you have your inhaler. I don't know why he's asking though. You haven't shown any asthmatic symptoms since you've been with us. Have you noticed that? Isn't that weird, since we're not clean freaks like you and your mom?"

I patted my pocket, where she could clearly see the outline of the inhaler. "You're right. I hadn't noticed that. That *is* weird."

Kendra pointed at the rides. "That, that, and then . . ." She turned to the Ferris wheel. "We're definitely doing that."

"I don't know."

"You don't need to know. Come on," she said, pulling me toward the carnival entrance so we could get our tickets.

A kid bumped into me and kept going, holding his stomach.

"Excuse us. Too many funnel cakes," his mother said, hurrying after him.

The intermingling scents of popcorn, hotdogs, and pretzels were overpowering. Kendra looked all around, trying to decide which fair food to splurge on first.

"I want some cotton candy," she finally decided. "I saw some back there."

"Go ahead. I'll wait here," I said.

"Are you sure?"

"Yeah, I don't want any."

"Be right back. Don't go anywhere."

"Where would I go?" I leaned against the wall of a kiddy water game and stared at my feet. *I should be here with my mom.* We came every year and had so much fun. Kendra was often with us. One year, we attended the carnival every single night. That was the best.

I looked up, hearing a familiar laugh. Pool was walking a few feet ahead, maneuvering around groups of carnival goers, his fingers interlocked with a girl's. He pulled her closer and wrapped his arm around her waist.

Either Tiffany Lancaster was finally showing her face, or Pool had a new conquest.

Raine would tell me to follow them, I knew he would, so I did.

The girl pointed at something, and they turned, just enough for me to see her profile. My mouth dropped. *Teresa? And she's not wearing anything orange?*

This couldn't be happening. She hated Pool. We'd talked about him on several occasions since the swamp party incident, when I called to check on her. She had to know that Tiffany didn't do it alone. Pool helped set her up with those embarrassing photos. How could she be so foolish? She'd even pulled me into this mess.

Then I remembered what Pool told me when he asked me to talk to Teresa so Tiffany could still graduate. "If you don't, then I will handle it myself," he had said. At the time, I didn't understand what he meant.

A part of me said to mind my business, that Teresa couldn't be stupid enough to believe Pool liked her. Or maybe she just craved attention, no matter who it came from. But as they moved away from me, toward the screams coming from the kiddie roller coaster, I followed. I stayed just far enough away that I could watch them through the crowd without being noticed.

Pool whispered in Teresa's ear, and they stopped at the giant Ferris wheel. It towered above everything. Vibrant neon lights started at a center point and spread outward like the rays of the sun, pulsating in a kaleidoscope of colors. The lights along the spokes of the wheel displayed dazzling patterns, glimmering to the beat of the music.

Pool kissed the side of Teresa's head as he looked past her. He paused there for a moment, as if studying something, and then handed over their tickets and climbed into a passenger car.

"One more for this one," said a girl before the guy locked the brace in front of them.

My eyes widened. Tiffany Lancaster went through the turnstile and squeezed in beside Teresa with a mischievous smirk.

The shock showed on Teresa's face. The man, in desperate need of a shave and possibly a drink, locked in the bar and the car lurched forward so he could load the next pod.

I moved into plain view, watching Teresa between Pool and Tiffany. Our eyes met briefly as her seat lifted higher, a millisecond that felt like an eternity. If only I could pause time and rescue her from that friggin pod or turn back time and prevent her from ever stepping foot on the Ferris wheel in the first place.

As soon as they reached the top, the ride stopped. Teresa was stuck up there while the operator took his time letting additional riders on. And there was nothing I could do about it.

I couldn't imagine what was about to happen, but I was still standing there when their pod finally descended. It took several minutes for the wheel to make one full rotation, the pods moving like the second hand of a clock. I could see Teresa's face clearly as they came down the other side. Her mascara was running, and tears streamed down her face.

I sprinted over to the ride operator, trying my best to look authoritative and not like a scrawny sixteen-year-old. "Excuse me, sir, but you need to bring them down!" I pointed. "Something is wrong. That girl is having a breakdown up there. I think she's sick."

There was a high-pitched scream. "What was that?" The ride operator's face paled as he looked up.

"Or do you want a lawsuit?"

With a shaky nod, he brought them down. Teresa was slumped over, unconscious. Pool and Tiffany leapt from the car and tried to run off, but I stepped in front of them, blocking their exit.

"I saw you," was all I said.

"Go," he told Tiffany, and they ran.

"Come back here! Stop them," yelled the ride attendant. Another carnival employee called for medical assistance.

Teresa's eyes were closed, her cheeks wet with tears.

"Is there a doctor here?" I shouted, frantically looking around for help.

"Here! I am!"

I turned and saw a spritely man with gray hair hurry over to us. "Please, help her," I pleaded, my voice shaking.

The man knelt beside Teresa and checked her pulse. He looked up at me with concern. "We need to get her off this ride immediately."

The carnival employee assisted as they carefully lifted Teresa out of the seat. The man introduced himself as Dr. Turner and told me he would do all he could, but they needed an ambulance.

It wasn't long before the ambulance drove right onto the park grounds, clearing a path through an aisle of games.

The paramedics forced us back so we couldn't see everything they were doing, but they carried Teresa away on a stretcher. Officers approached and questioned the ride operator until he pointed at me. Another officer joined them, and while they were distracted, I slinked away into the crowd and searched for Kendra.

"Where the heck have you been? Did you see what happened over there?" she asked, pointing behind her at the Ferris wheel.

"Someone got hurt," I replied.

"You saw?"

I nodded slowly. I don't know why, but she pulled me aside. Maybe I was doing a terrible job of hiding how upset I was.

"This is a small town. Was it someone we know?" she asked.

"Teresa."

"No way. T-Bird Teresa?"

I nodded. "An ambulance just took her away."

"Are you kidding?"

"I wish I was. Can you call your dad to pick us up?"

When we got to school the next day, Tiffany Lancaster was waiting out in the grid, looking around all anxious. She caught me right as I was getting out of Kendra's truck.

I tried to ignore her as I walked by.

"Hey, Storm?"

I rolled my eyes and turned to face her. "Yeah?"

"You don't have to act all salty. I just wanted to tell you that I don't know what you saw, but I didn't do anything."

"Oh, please," I scoffed. "I know you, Tiffany, and I know why you were jealous of Teresa."

Kendra was silent but stayed close, her arm grazing mine as if to say, "I'm here if you need me."

"I wasn't jealous!" Tiffany shot back.

"Are you sure about that? The whole school thinks differently, and we all know why—because Pool liked Teresa, and you saw that he did. I even witnessed your boyfriend drooling over her cleavage. So, because of a boy, you plotted against her. And this time, wouldn't you know it, I just happened to be there to witness the whole thing."

Tiffany stood there glaring at me. Her lips tightened and her face turned red. I walked away.

"Yeah," said Kendra and followed me.

At lunch, Tiffany and her crew gave me the side-eye. As usual, they had no volume control, so I was close enough to hear them in passing.

"She's a good girl. She won't say anything. Good girls don't tell. Isn't that what they say?"

"Not in that context," said someone else.

I pushed my tray away and stood up from the cafeteria table. "I'm going to head out," I told Kendra. She began to stand. "No, finish your lunch. I'm going to class."

No one had witnessed what I had at the carnival. I didn't want to be anywhere near Tiffany Lancaster or Pool. But as I walked through the crowded hallway, I heard footsteps behind me.

"If you were going to tell, you would've already," said Pool.

I pretended not to hear him and kept walking.

"This makes us cool again."

I shook my head. "We were never cool."

28

After school, I got picked up, then dropped off at the hospital. Although she wasn't around, Mr. J would not stray from my mother's routine and picked me up every day. If I didn't know any better, I'd guess she had also called and instructed him to make sure I had my inhalers and kept the air purifier running in Kendra's bedroom.

A nurse walked in and wrote her name on the chalkboard on the wall across from us. I clutched my mother's hand, cold under my touch.

"Stormie?" my mom said.

"Ma'am?"

"Let's go home."

"Really? They've discharged you?"

She nodded with a grin. "Close the door, so I can get dressed."

What had seemed like suicide was deemed an accidental overdose. Relief swept over me when I heard those words. My mother wasn't trying to kill herself, and it wasn't because of my actions. She had taken too many pills for her different ailments. Additional pills that I didn't know she was taking.

Note to self: Keep closer tabs on her meds.

As soon as we got down to the lobby, I checked my mother's rideshare app and saw our car had arrived. That was a relief; I wouldn't have to listen to her complain about waiting in the discharge lounge.

Once we were home, I went into full "mom mode", making sure she ate some soup, then made sure she was comfy in bed. When she finally fell asleep, I video called Kendra to tell her we were back.

"I know you're glad she's home," said Kendra.

"Yeah, but now we have weekly doctor visits to make sure she's not cuckoo for Cocoa Puffs."

Kendra laughed. "This is not the time to make cereal jokes."

"I know, too soon. Bad joke."

"Seriously, do they think something is wrong?"

"No, they are being cautious. It's their procedure to continue to examine her mental state. That's what my mom said, anyway."

Kendra's smile faded, and the weight of the situation settled between us. "I hope she's okay."

"Me too," I muttered, feeling a tightness in my chest that wasn't just from the asthma.

I wanted to believe my mother when she said everything was fine, but I kept a close eye on her just in case. I organized her medications, made sure she took them on time, and monitored her moods, keeping a record of it all in my journal.

At first, she seemed like my normal mom. She went back to work and resumed her routine. But as we got closer to graduation, I started noticing she was becoming more irritable and prone to angry outbursts over minor things. She spent more and more time alone in her room just staring at the television, oblivious to what she was watching.

I tried talking to her, asking her how she was feeling, but she always insisted she was fine.

One night, I woke to the sound of crying. I stayed still for a moment making sure that was what I was hearing. Then I hopped up, ran to my mother's room, and found her hunched over at the edge of her bed, shoulders shaking with each tear that fell.

My heart broke seeing her like that. This wasn't my strong, capable mother. I sat with her, holding her, allowing her to cry as much as she needed to.

When the sobs finally subsided, she looked at me with red-rimmed eyes. "I'm so tired," she whispered. "It's just been too much—for too long."

"What's too much?" I asked as I held her close. I looked off to the left, seeing her closet door open and the gun safe on the floor with envelopes strewn all around it.

"It's going to be okay," I told her. "Do you know how many times you have told me that after every asthma attack and every trip to the hospital? I always believed you. Now you have to believe me."

She nodded and sniffed.

I dried her eyes with the tissue she held. "Forgive me for rubbing snot in your lashes."

That made her laugh. We stayed awake talking early into the morning. But not once did she mention what I really wanted to talk about. The letters were still on the floor, and I acted like they were invisible.

Later that morning, I went to her bedroom as soon as I woke up. The gun safe was back up on the shelf, and the letters were nowhere to be seen. I found Mom in the kitchen, once again, making breakfast like nothing had happened.

"Good morning, Stormie," she said brightly as I entered. "Pancakes?"

"Pancakes? What about tea?"

"We've got that too. Is that a yes?"

"Mom, I would never turn down pancakes."

She set a plate of three pancakes with crispy edges, just the way I liked them, in front of me. We ate in silence. I studied her face for any traces of the deep sorrow I had witnessed the night before. But she seemed calm, even cheerful.

After breakfast, she gave me a quick peck on the cheek and headed upstairs while I cleaned up the dishes. Clearly, she was in denial and unwilling to talk about what was causing her so much pain.

When I finished cleaning up, I called up the stairs, "Mom, can I ride to the hospital with you to see my friend? Over the school announcements they had said that she was conscious."

"Yes, of course."

The blinds were drawn in Teresa's room. I walked in, but didn't speak. At first, I thought she was asleep. She didn't make a sound and wouldn't turn in my direction.

"Teresa?"

She slowly turned her head, and I walked closer to her bed. I don't know what I expected her to do when she saw me, but she didn't smile. For a moment, I wasn't certain she even recognized me. She was emotionless and pale, replaced with a hard, uncaring clone.

"I need your help," she finally said.

"Of course, anything," I replied as I sat beside her.

Her voice was just above a whisper. "I have a plan. I'm going to get them back for what they did to me."

"What?" Her statement caught me off guard. "What are you talking about?"

"Revenge."

How could she be thinking about that right now? This wasn't the Teresa I knew.

"You think you know what I've been through, but you don't. What you didn't see, and what I haven't shared, was how I was harassed at school by their friends. One of them kicked me in the back while I was walking and threw food at me."

"What? Teresa, I didn't know."

"Of course you didn't. Everyone likes you. You're the 'good girl.' Well, they didn't feel the same about me. And those who had liked me turned on me. I met this boy online, on one of those messaging apps. We had been chatting a lot, and I went to meet him secretly without my parents knowing. We planned to meet up near the Fun House at the carnival. I waited, but he didn't show. You know who did show? Pool.

He asked me if I was looking for Eric, and when I said yes, he gave an obnoxious bow. He went on to repeat all the details of my private conversations with 'Eric'"—her hands raised to air quote the fake name— "But then he had the nerve to try and convince me that he'd made up the account because he really liked me and didn't want Tiffany to find out.

"Well, I fell for it. Then, he gave me a gummy. Many, actually."

"You don't mean—"

"Yeah, edibles. But I didn't know what they were. I mentioned they were kind of bitter. Pool said it was because they were all natural and homemade. I think the delayed effect made Pool keep giving them to me because I wasn't reacting right away." Teresa squeezed her eyes shut. "But then I started feeling dizzy and out of it—intoxicated. That's why I got on that ride. I don't even like heights. And then Tiffany showed up. It wasn't a coincidence. They planned the whole thing—to poison me, to cause an overdose," she said and looked towards the window.

I waited for her to tell me what happened next. She hadn't mentioned why she screamed up there. Perhaps she couldn't remember. I pictured her fighting for her life to keep them from throwing her off the ride.

"I have a plan," she finally said. "I've put everything in place for graduation. It's all in that notebook right there, as well as the names of the others involved. I just need your help with it."

"Help with what?"

She looked away from the window, her blue eyes filling with tears as she looked into mine. She pointed at the notebook. "Whatever happens, promise me you will make sure it all goes down."

"I . . ." I didn't know what to say or what she was talking about. "I don't—"

"It has to be you. You saw them. They'll come after you too—that I'm sure of. Make them pay, Storm. For me. If our friendship ever meant anything to you . . ."

"What are you asking me to do?"

"It's time to change the narrative."

"How?"

She lowered her voice as the nurse came into the room and stopped at the sink.

"You saw what they did to me. Did you tell anyone it was them?"

I shook my head.

"Then you are just as guilty as they are. You owe me."

I stared at her, stunned. What the heck was she asking me to do? Revenge had never crossed my mind. I just wanted her to get better.

"I—I can't do that," I stammered. "I won't hurt anyone, if that's what you're asking. That won't solve anything."

She grabbed my hand, her eyes blazing. "You're a good person, always have been. But they need to pay—them, their friends. The whole school needs to understand that actions have consequences."

Her intensity frightened me. This wasn't her. Or had this dark side lurked beneath the surface all along?

"Please, Teresa," I begged. "Let's focus on getting you well. We can talk to the principal and get Pool and Tiffany expelled—"

She cut me off with a hollow laugh. "Expelled? Is that all you think they deserve after what they did? After they took my life from me?"

"Took your life? I'm not sure I understand," I said. "Can you walk me through it?"

"There's no time," she whispered, glancing at the nurse. "Just know that graduation is the day it will happen. You make sure it does."

My mouth went dry.

Teresa squeezed my hand with surprising strength. Her eyes bore intensely into mine. "You're the only one I can trust. Promise me you'll do this."

I hesitated, then gave a small nod. Her grip relaxed and she settled back into the pillows.

"Good. Now take the notebook and go."

I slowly rose from my seat, slid the notebook into my bag, and glanced at Teresa one last time, but she focused on the window again.

What had I just agreed to?

29

In a dimly lit corner of the only cafe in Spencer besides Starbucks, the faint scent of freshly roasted coffee beans mingled with the aroma of the danishes and cookies in the display case. I was locked in a silent standoff with a toddler at another table. His unblinking gaze held a challenge, an unspoken test of who could stare the longest. I blinked, and he continued to stare.

The cafe was across the street from the hospital, where I told my mother I would meet her. I opened my backpack and pulled out Teresa's notebook. Doodles of everything from lipstick to candles as well as the words "Senior Project," decorated the orange cover. I was hesitant about opening it. Maybe the secrets it held needed to remain just that—secrets.

The moment I opened the book, I knew I had just agreed to something terrifying.

Inside, I found names and phone numbers and various notes I didn't understand about pyrotechnics. But then I ran my finger along something I *did* understand.

I gasped and grabbed my composition notebook from my backpack—the one I kept the notes in about my dream. I flipped to the page that listed the signs that led to the end of the world. I put the notebooks side by side and read:

My dream: *The Crimson Star Ascends*

Teresa's notes: *Red balloon*

My dream: *The Heavens Weep*

Teresa's notes: *The sky cries*

My dream: *Gravity Unshackled*

Teresa's notes: *Gravity falls*

My dream: *The Writhing Plague*

Teresa's notes: *Worms*

My dream: *The Day of Reckoning*

Teresa's notes: *Judgment day*

My dream: *The Dead Walk Among Us*

Teresa's notes: *Return from the dead*

My dream: *Final Dawn*

Teresa's notes: *The end*

What is happening? How is this possible? My hand covered my mouth and was still there when my mother shook me. I hadn't heard or seen arrive.

"Stormie, what's wrong?" She sat beside me, focused on my face, and pushed my hand down. "What happened? Are you holding your breath? Breathe, Storm."

That was the last thing I heard. The last thing I remembered seeing was a blurry kid staring at me from another table.

The next thing I knew, I was lying on a hospital bed, looking up at the white tiles of the emergency room ceiling.

"It's a good thing we were across the street from the hospital," I murmured. "Did they shoot me up with the good stuff this time?" I joked. "The steroids? I feel fine."

"No, Storm. It wasn't an attack this time," my mom said. "You fainted."

30

—·—

I left the hospital in a daze. What had I done? I tried to remember. *Did I actually say, "Yes, I will do this" when Teresa asked?* Was I really willing to go through with her plan? I didn't even understand what the plan was.

My mother didn't probe me with questions on the way home. I'm sure she wanted to, but I hugged myself and leaned my head against the window with my eyes closed.

As we walked through the front door, I stopped her from hovering by telling her I was going to take a nap. I locked my bedroom door, pulled the notebook from my bag (thankfully she had grabbed all my things), and flicked through the pages, most of them filled with Teresa's loopy handwriting.

Toward the back of the book, the tone shifted. The writing became darker, angrier. She described Pool and Tiffany's bullying in excruciating detail—the daily torments that had pushed her to the edge. There were lists of supplies, diagrams of the school, and schedules of when certain teachers and students would be where.

My heart sank as I realized just how methodical her plan was. *Was my dream trying to warn me about Teresa?*

This was too big for me. I contemplated discussing it with my mother, Teresa's counselor, Mrs. Fisher, or the principal, but I had made a promise. She trusted me to help. Still, the thought of actually going through with it made me nauseous.

I sat there for a long time, staring at the notebook. This wasn't just about revenge for Teresa anymore. Pool and Tiffany had bullied others, too, and Teresa was taking a stand. She wanted justice not just for herself, but for everyone they had hurt.

And while I agreed with her on that, how far was this going to go? There was so much that I didn't understand in her writing. On one page was a scrawled paragraph:

They think I'm weak. They think I'm invisible, that their words don't stab me—little cuts which have led to a slow, agonizing death. But they don't know what I've been planning, what I've been building inside. Every insult, every shove, every mocking laugh—it all adds up. I've been pushed to the edge, and they have no idea what's coming. They'll see the real me, the one they've tried to bury beneath their cruelty. This will be my release. This will set me free.

"This will set me free," I repeated, interpreting the writing as the anguished poetry of a depressed teenager that has lost all hope and faith. Closing the notebook, I turned to my laptop and opened a search engine. My fingers hovered over the keys as I considered my options. Finally, I typed: *How to stop a revenge plot.*

Most of the results had the same answer: Give it time.

Give it time? How the heck is that supposed to help?

Kendra kept texting, asking if I was okay. Finally, I responded: *Resting.*

I went back to Teresa's notebook. One page was marked with a date and time, circled in red ink. In large, bold letters, the words **BE THERE** were written and underlined multiple times. A rush of nerves hit me as I realized this was for me.

A few days later, I went, unsure what I was walking into or if anyone else would show.

Rick, the sound guy for the podcast, walked toward me, waved, and leaned against the wall. Then, three others arrived and stood beside him, their faces serious.

Marching band members walked in and out of the band room. Drumsticks hit against snares, and several horns blew.

"Storm, are you waiting for someone?" Rick called over the noise.

"I'm here for a meeting."

He flicked his head back to maneuver the hair hanging over his eye. "What meeting?"

I'm going to take a chance that they are here for the same meeting, I thought and walked over to their side of the hall. "Teresa's meeting," I whispered.

They all glanced at each other and back at me.

"She brought you into this too?" Rick asked.

"Yeah."

They were silent, as if they didn't know what to say next.

"What now?" I asked.

"Wait and see if she told anyone else," said Rick.

We stood there for a while as a couple of boys walked by talking about some summer drum and bugle corps.

"Hey, have you ever watched—" a girl started.

I cut her off. "You know, we don't have to do that thing where we try to connect by finding something we have in common. This is not that type of meetup. We're all here for the same reason, to help Teresa. Although, I'm not sure I want to be part of whatever she planned."

"You don't know what we're doing? Then why are you here?" she asked.

"Because I think I owe it to her."

"Why?" asked the boy wearing a slouchy beanie with short dreadlocks hanging under it. I'd seen him in a class or two over the years, but we never really spoke before.

I bit my lip. "Teresa knows."

They exchanged looks.

"Does everyone else have a notebook like this?" I asked, raising Teresa's doodled notebook in the air.

"No. What's that?"

"Teresa gave it to me the other day."

Rick flipped through the pages. "Probably because you're late to the party. We've been working on this for a while," he replied and handed it back to me.

I pointed at the notebook. "So you know what this senior project is then?"

"Oh, one hundred percent."

"Then what does she need me for?"

"Only you know the answer to that."

"She said she wanted me to make sure it happens. Make sure what happens?"

"Retribution," said the girl.

"But—"

"Storm! Hey!"

"Mrs. Caplan?"

She power walked toward me wearing a shirt dress with leggings. I think she had the outfit in every color. "I'm so glad I ran into you. Storm, I still need your paper, but I know you're waiting on the DNA results, and I agree with you—the DNA information will really make your paper shine. But I need you to hightail it over to me as soon as it arrives, okay?

You have an A in the class, you know that already, but this grade is still important.".

"I will," I replied, watching Rick and the others walk away. Mrs. Caplan had already given me the A for what I turned in because grades were due. But I wasn't sure if she wanted to make sure I completed the paper or if she was just as interested as I was in finding out the DNA results.

"I'm expecting it any day. It won't be hard to finish once I get the results."

"That's good to hear," Mrs. Caplan said and darted away. She wasn't in a hurry to get somewhere, she just always walked like that.

Retribution. I knew it meant payback, but I pulled out my phone and looked up the definition. "Punishment imposed for purposes of repayment or revenge for the wrong committed."

The next, I was sitting in economics class when the whispers around me grew louder with each student who entered the room.

"What's going on?" I asked the girl closest to me.

She leaned over. "That girl that something happened to at the carnival, Teresa, isn't coming back to school."

"Uh huh," said the boy behind me, who was reading something on his phone and then placed it in his pocket. "It's worse than that. She died."

I gasped.

"Some people are saying it was suicide," added another student from across the room.

A lump formed in my throat and tears stung my eyes. This couldn't be happening—not to someone I knew.

Our teacher walked in and stood at her desk in silence for a moment. "Class, I'm sure you've all heard about Teresa's passing."

The room fell silent.

"I want each one of you to know that if you're struggling with anything, there is always someone who cares and is willing to listen. Please reach out for help if you need it."

As she spoke about mental health and the resources available for students, I couldn't help but wonder why Teresa didn't reach out for help. Did she feel like there was no one who cared? Did she think I didn't care?

We didn't have much of a lesson that day and when the bell rang, everyone packed up their things without a word and left the classroom.

I walked out into the hall, not really paying attention to anyone. When I reached my next class, a group of students were huddling together, talking and laughing outside of the door. It was Pool and some of his fan club.

"Good riddance," he said as I approached.

Before I could stop myself, I slapped him.

He lunged at me, but his friends held him back

I threw my backpack down. "Evil friggen scumbag," I shouted at him.

He laughed. "Such a good girl. Is that the worst you can say? You can't even curse right."

"Don't worry, you're going to get yours," I told him.

"Ooo . . . I'm so scared."

Mrs. Fisher saw it all. She picked up my bag and grabbed me, pulling me away.

"Yo, she slapped the crap out of you," said one of Pool's friends.

Mrs. Fisher dragged me down to her office, and as soon as I walked in, Teresa's senior photo stared back at me.

I paced back and forth in front of her.

"Storm, calm down." Her expression was a mix of worry and what almost looked like pride, like she was concerned but also proud of me for standing up for myself. "Sit," she said.

I plopped onto the sofa, and Mrs. Fisher sat across from me. "What happened out there?" she asked.

"He was making fun of Teresa's death."

"So I gathered, but was slapping him really the best way to handle it?"

"I reacted without thinking. It was blind anger."

She handed me a tissue. "It's understandable that you're upset. Hell, I'm upset."

I blinked a few times. Did she really just say "H-e-dou-ble-hockey-stick"?

"But violence isn't the answer. What if his friends didn't or couldn't hold him back? You and I probably wouldn't be in this office right now, we'd be in a hospital room."

"The story of my life," I mumbled. I wiped away my tears and nodded in agreement. "But you're right, I'm sorry." I grabbed my backpack from the floor.

"Wait. Just hold on a minute, I'll email your teacher. Stay here and relax for a while."

I sat back down. Maybe that's what made Mrs. Fisher a great counselor—she understood that what I needed right then was to avoid facing my classmates. The rest of the day went by in a blur, and Pool's vehement dislike for me seemed to be spreading like a virus through the senior class. I wasn't imagining it; the glares and snickers that followed me were proof enough.

In the midst of all that was happening, Kendra kept texting: *Storm, pick up!* But I wasn't in the mood to talk to anyone.

The whole school knew about Teresa, and by the end of the day, they probably all knew about the slap.

I lay on my bed that night, curled my legs tightly into my chest, and cried.

Mrs. Fisher had called my mother, so she knew what happened and had comforted me as best she could, but I just wanted to be alone.

Late into the night, my phone wouldn't stop vibrating, so I checked it.

Kendra: *I kicked Pool in the nuts!*

I sat up: *What?*

Kendra: *He may not be able to have kids now.*

I dropped the phone, punched at the air, and pounded my feet on the bed! *Yes!* Kendra always had my back.

Kendra: *And when he fell forward, I planted a kiss on his forehead. Girl, it was salty.*

Me: *See, this is why I love you.*

Kendra: *Are you okay? Because I need to tell you something.*

Me: *I will be. What's up?*

Kendra: *I'm going to prom.*

I sat up and wiped my eyes. *With who?*

Kendra: *Ramen boy.*

Me: *Bryson?*

Kendra: *The one and only. I thought he liked you. Turns out he liked me. Is that okay? If you like him, I'll tell him no.*

Was it okay? Kendra was my best friend, of course it was okay. I guess that meant that Bryson was only being nice to me because it was his job, or for tips, or because he wanted me to say nice things about him to Kendra. I think it was the latter. Good for her.

Kendra: *Now we can go together.*

Me: *Uh . . .*

Kendra: *Don't say it.*

Me*: I'm not going.*

Kendra: *I knew it. Why?*

Me: *Because of Teresa. I don't feel right celebrating anything. The school should have canceled it. But you go and have a good time.*

Kendra: *Then I'm not going either.*

Me: *Are you crazy? You go and have the most amazing time—for both of us.*

I was happy for Kendra. Although my mom might have a fit about it, since she liked Bryson so much. I leaned back against my headboard. Would Teresa care that I was boycotting the prom? What about her plan, now that she was gone? Maybe that's why she wanted me to make sure it was carried out. She knew she wouldn't be here.

My anger subsided as I prayed for forgiveness—for slapping Pool and for the hatred I felt. I still didn't like him. How could I ever forgive him?

But what would it all matter when high school—and the world—were coming to an end? Or was it all just coming down to Teresa's senior project?

31

— · —

The countdown to graduation was ticking away like a time bomb and, at this point, I had no idea what the outcome would be. The days were shifting from warm to hot, mosquitoes were on the warpath, and it was still only spring.

My mom seemed to be doing okay. I hadn't checked for any more red envelopes, and there were no more appearances from the tall guy. All I could think about was Teresa and awaited information about her funeral.

I distracted myself by helping Kendra find a prom dress.

Kendra was thrilled when I texted her about it, so we made plans to meet at the mall after school. Spencer didn't have a mall. We had to drive approximately thirty minutes by highway to get to the nearest one. And, as predicted, my mother freaked out when she found out that Bryson was taking Kendra to prom instead of me.

"Storm! Why didn't you tell him you wanted to go with him?" she exclaimed as we drove.

"It's fine, Mom. He wasn't interested in me. He was into Kendra. Plus, I told Kendra I didn't want to go anyway."

"What? Why not?"

I hesitated before answering and looked away. "Because of Teresa."

Mom reached over to squeeze my hand. "I understand."

We arrived at Chesterfield mall, and I texted Kendra: *We're here!* We always met outside the same set of doors at the back of the mall. Kendra ran out waving, and I got out of the car. "Meet you at the food court," my mom yelled.

"Okay!" we both yelled back.

"Took you long enough to get here," said Kendra. "Now do you think she's really going to wait at the food court or is she going to follow us."

"You know she's going to follow us."

We laughed as we hurried inside. "I know exactly where to go first!" said Kendra. She talked non-stop and led me straight to the prom dress section of one of our favorite stores. I followed her around as she pulled dresses from the racks and handed them to me, going on and on about being flawless for the prom.

I smiled as I watched her try them on and twirl in front of the mirror. She looked beautiful in every single one of them, but ultimately decided on an emerald-green strapless gown with a sparkly bodice.

Kendra placed her hands on her waist and sucked in her stomach. "Bryson is going to have to wear a matching suit or tux. I don't know where he is going to find one this color, but he'd better get on it."

I grinned. "I'm sure he will."

"What do you think? Green nails?"

"Not the whole nail. French, with a little sparkle."

"See, that's why we are friends. You know me."

Next, we found her a pair of strappy heels, and to my surprise, she didn't walk any better than I did in them. But Kendra practiced in them every day while Mom and I watched and tried to help. She also wore them while vacuuming and doing dishes, so that by prom night, she could dance all night long—or at least until curfew.

The night of the prom, I helped Kendra get ready like a mother would help her daughter get ready for her wedding, at least based on what I'd seen in movies. The green dress hugged her figure perfectly and complimented the warm tones of her skin. Her long hair, styled in loose, cascading waves, was pinned back on one side with a jeweled clip that matched her dress. It had been so long since I had seen Kendra without braids. I had no idea her hair was so long.

"Don't get used to it, this is just for tonight" she groaned and fanned herself. "It's entirely too hot for anything but braids," she said and backed up to the window. I followed her gaze and watched Bryson step out of his car, sporting an emerald-green tie and vest under his black tux.

"This is really happening," Kendra sang, her eyes wide as she clasped my hand.

"Don't mess up your makeup. Go show Bryson how amazing you look. Beauty and brains, whew!"

I followed Kendra outside, carefully holding her dress to keep it from brushing the ground, and I'll never forget the look on Bryson's face when he saw her. Mostly because I don't think a boy had ever looked at me that way. I might as well have been watching a scene from a romantic movie. Bryson's eyes widened, and for a moment, he just stood there, unmoving. Then his mouth parted slightly, as if he wanted to say something but forgot how to speak. There was a mix of awe and disbelief in his expression. A slow, stunned smile crept onto his face, and I could almost see him taking in every detail—the way Kendra's dress shimmered, the soft curls of her hair, and the glow in her eyes. He looked like cupid had struck him.

"You—you're gorgeous," he finally said, blushing.

"You better make this the best night of her life," I told him, though I wasn't sure of exactly how threatening I sounded.

Mr. J took about a thousand pictures, and I backed away and watched until he made me join them in a few.

"It's hot out here!" Kendra exclaimed.

I motioned to Bryson. "Please get her in the car before the humidity ruins her hair and makeup."

"Oh yeah, of course," he said and carefully ushered her away.

After Kendra and Bryson left, Mr. J dropped me off at home, and I spent the rest of the afternoon holed up in my room, trying to avoid my mom's questions about what was wrong. I was still adamant about not going to prom, but to be honest, I felt like I might be missing out on something great.

It was a poor replacement for not going to prom, but I decided to make the evening a "me night" filled with movies and junk food. But as soon as I grabbed my snacks and settled on what series I would binge watch for the night, the rumble of a motorcycle grew louder, then it stopped outside my house. I looked out of my window and hurried downstairs.

"Who's that?" Mom asked.

"I don't know," I yelled behind me.

I opened the front door and stood there for a moment looking, in case it was the tall man. But it wasn't.

Raine sat on his bike with his helmet lens raised. "Hey," he said, as I approached.

"Hey," I replied, trying to sound nonchalant. "What are you doing here?"

He patted the seat behind him. "Hop on."

"Nope. Not doing that. Do you know how many motorcycle accidents—"

Raine squinted and tilted his head.

"Oh, I'm doing that 'random facts' thing again, aren't I?"

He nodded and lifted a helmet at me. "Live a little. Before the end of the world."

That got my attention. I hesitated for a moment and looked back at my house. My mom had come out onto the porch. I put my index finger first and then made prayer hands.

She shook her head slightly. I could hear her in my head: *Storm, don't you dare.*

Before the end of the world, I told myself and climbed onto the back of Raine's bike. This was so unlike me, but I was doing it. I put on the helmet Raine handed me and wrapped my arms around his waist before my mom could run over and snatch me off.

Raine revved the motorcycle, and we took off down the road. I was anxious at first, but then decided to be intentional about enjoying the moment. I leaned forward against Rain and lifted my arms out to the sides. I felt free, and all my worries seemed to fade away.

He didn't go too fast at first. I think that was for my sake. Maybe he could tell I had never ridden on a motorcycle before.

We drove through winding roads until we reached the highway. I held on tight, excited for an adventure and happy to get away from everything I knew.

Soon, traffic picked up and I noticed highway signs for Atlanta. *Where is he taking me?*

We were at least an hour from home when Raine pulled us off the highway and stopped at a large white house. The property looked as though it could have been a plantation at one time. It was now dusk, and there were lights on inside the house.

A woman walked out on the front porch as Raine took off his helmet, shook his curls, and helped me off the motorcycle.

He waved, took my hand, and we walked up to the woman with the darkest ebony complexion and her hair wrapped in a scarf that made her look like an African queen. "Hey, Sugarfoot!" she exclaimed.

I giggled. "Sugar what? Where exactly are we?"

"Storm," he said, guiding me in front of him, "this is my grandmother, Nya."

"So this is the Storm I've heard so much about."

Raine has talked about me? I hoped she didn't see the shock on my face. *Don't turn red, don't turn red*, I chanted in my head.

She acted jealous, but I could tell she was joking.

"Grandma, you know you're the only lady in my life."

"Yeah, right."

I reached out to shake her hand, but she pulled me into a hug.

"Welcome to my home, Storm. Come on inside, you two."

We followed her. "Raine, I'm confused. Is this your girlfriend, Nya, who lives in Atlanta?"

Raine nodded with a mischievous grin. "Oh, you've heard that?" he laughed. "I'm here all the time, helping out. And we're not exactly in Atlanta." His grandmother's house had a good feeling, and the best fragrances. It felt like a place I would want to be.

Before I could take a step forward, Raine stepped in front of me, blocking my view. "Are we ready?" he asked his grandmother.

"We sure are," she replied.

"Good." Raine faced me and whipped a handkerchief out of his pocket.

"What are you about to do with that? Am I about to be taken? My mother has a very particular set of skills . . ."

"You're quoting the movie *Taken* right now?"

"I'm actually quoting Liam Neeson's character in *Taken*."

"Just trust me."

"All right," I said. "I hope I won't regret this."

"You won't."

I closed my eyes and Raine tied the handkerchief behind my head, blindfolding me, and led me forward.

A door squealed open. "Watch your step," Raine said as my foot hung in the air, and I realized I was stepping down.

Once my feet were on the ground, he walked me out a little farther. "Okay. Stop here."

"Okay," I replied.

"Don't open your eyes," Raine said as he took the blindfold off.

I kept my eyes shut, wondering why I was shaking. Maybe it was because no one had tried to surprise me before.

He turned me around so that I was facing something. "Okay, open your eyes."

I hesitated. I didn't understand what this was. What was he trying to accomplish? Finally, I stopped overthinking and opened them.

My hands shot to my mouth, seeing a tunnel of greenery arches adorned with fairy lights lighting a path to the garden on the other side.

Raine held his hand out. "Welcome to your prom."

I took his hand and walked under the tunnel. On the other side there had to be at least twenty faux trees covered in twinkling lights. Drapes of white fabric connected the flower-covered wall panels. Smooth jazz music suddenly switched on, and not far from us was a table with a white tablecloth. Two place settings were all set up, with silverware and plates that looked way too fancy for us.

"I don't understand. How did you do all of this? *Why* did you do all of this?"

"I wanted to make sure you had a great prom night, something good to remember from senior year." He led me to the table. "It makes sense why you're not going with the rest of those wipeouts. I just wanted to do this for you."

"But how?" I looked up and around. Even the stars were making a supportive appearance. "This had to be expensive. You're not rich."

"You don't know what I am. Plus, I know people who own things and don't mind helping out a family member for a good cause."

"Oh, so I'm a cause?"

"Yes, you're the girl who needs to have more experiences before the end of the world."

"Well, I can't disagree with that."

It was probably the greatest night of my life—there, on Raine's grandmother's farm, with incredible decorations, food and dancing. *He likes me. This whole time, he liked me*, I thought.

Even though he never said it, and didn't ask me to be his girlfriend or try to kiss me, I knew he liked me. And, based on everything he did to make the night possible, he must have liked me a whole lot.

I was so thankful and grateful for him that I was on an incredible high the entire evening.

Before we left, Raine's grandmother hugged him like she might never see him again.

"Are you okay?" he asked.

She nodded. "Be good, Sugarfoot."

"Yes, ma'am. I will."

A truck pulled up into the driveway and a man got out and walked over.

"Hey, Unc." Raine said as the man started up the walk.

"You know I don't like you riding that motorcycle at night."

"I know, that's why I'm taking the car home. I'll come back for my bike tomorrow."

"Send your father. It's been a minute since he's been by. Is this her? Your girl?"

"Stop it," Raine told him. "This is my friend, Storm."

"Pleased to meet you, young lady."

"Hello," I said.

"See you at graduation," Raine told his grandmother.

"Ummm . . ." she replied and walked away.

"What was that about?" Raine asked. "Is she not coming?"

His uncle looked over his shoulder. "Oh, don't mind her. She's got it in her head that the world is ending."

32

My heart started beating faster. I had gone back and forth about whether or not my recurring dream was really just a dream until that moment. I couldn't believe what I was hearing.

"Jesus is coming for his church," Mrs. Nya proclaimed from the porch.

"I've never heard her say that before. She's serious about this. When does she think it's going to happen?" asked Raine.

His uncle lifted a brow.

"What?"

His uncle lowered his head, still looking at him.

"You mean the day of my graduation?"

I backed away. How could she know? That's the same date I was told in the dream. Before I knew it, tears streamed from my eyes. "It's real. It's going to happen."

"Get your girl," said Raine's uncle.

Raine turned to me. "Whoa, Storm. What's wrong?"

"N-nothing, It's okay. I just—can you take me home?"

We drove in silence all the way to my house, with Raine glancing over every now and then and me biting on a nail until my finger turned red.

Raine pulled into the driveway and shut the engine off.

"Raine—"

"Are you going to tell me what happened? Why did you freak-out?"

I knew what he was probably thinking. That I didn't appreciate all it took for him to put the night together. That I didn't appreciate *him*. I shook my head. "I'm so sorry. Tonight was actually the best night of my life. No one has ever done anything like that for me."

"Are you telling me you were overcome with emotion?"

Through the windshield, I watched my mom walk out on the porch, her arms crossed over her chest.

"I'm telling you that we can talk more about this later. I promise. But right now, as soon as I get out, leave."

He looked up at the house and started the car. "Okay, but we could just explain—"

"Not right now," I told him and quickly kissed him on the lips. I couldn't believe I did that, and we stared at each other for a moment, both looking shocked.

I hopped out of the car and walked up to the house as he pulled away.

"Storm Davis, do you know what I've been going through? You wouldn't pick up your phone! And I couldn't call Kendra because she's at the prom."

"Mom, I'm so sorry. I forgot my phone."

"Who was that? And where were you? You're not an adult, you can't just leave. Why did you leave like that in the first place? That's not like you."

"I—I don't know." I placed my hands over her folded arms, and she looked me in the eyes.

"You've been crying."

"Mom, his family made a prom for me in their backyard."

Her hand flew to her mouth. "Get inside and tell me every-thing. I'll figure out your punishment later."

We sat at the kitchen table and my mom held a fist to her mouth as I told her all about my evening. But I left out the part about the end of the world. She broke into tears and let out a gasp. "If that wasn't the most thoughtful, romantic thing I've ever heard. You deserved that and more, Storm."

"Then . . . I'm not grounded?" I asked, hopeful.

"Yeah, you're grounded for life. Just joking. You get a pass."

Graduation was three days later and during those 72 hours, I couldn't get up the nerve to call Raine. I didn't know what to say.

He didn't call me either. *Why did I have to kiss him?*

The night before graduation, I had two dreams. The first was about Teresa. We were standing in a dark hallway, and she glared at me. "You didn't try hard enough," she said. "You promised!"

My eyes shot open, and I lay there for a while, hugging my pillow and thinking about her before I drifted off again. Then, I dreamed of the mysterious man whose face I could never see. He kept his back to me as he spoke. "This is the last time I will come to you," he said.

"Come to me for what?"

"To remind you of the end."

"I don't believe the world is ending."

"It's your world that is ending," he exclaimed, then turned to face me. At the same time, the brightest light I have ever seen blocked him from view.

I woke up in a cold sweat, with sunlight streaming through my window. *It's graduation day, and the end of the world day, Storm. Whatever the day is going to bring, it's time to face it.*

I showered, dressed, and made an attempt at breakfast for me and my mom. I wasn't the greatest cook, but I tried my best to be quiet so I could surprise her. My phone pinged as I set a skillet on the stove.

It was an email notification. I grinned and texted Raine.

Me: *I got it.*

Raine: *No, not you too. Are you okay? Is it the flu? We need to talk.*

Me: *No, I got the DNA results.*

Raine: *What? Can you get up to the school early before graduation so we can record you reading the results?*

Me: *It's going to be tight.*

Raine: *You promised.*

Me and my promises, I thought to myself with a sigh.

Me: *You're right. I'll talk my mom into letting me come early and tell her I'll see her at graduation.*

Raine: *See you in a few minutes.* He meant that literally because I lived right down the street. Which meant he lived close by too.

I quickly called Kendra.

"Hello?" she groaned.

"Wake up! We've got to get to the school!"

"Is it time for graduation?" she mumbled.

"No. My DNA results are in. Raine wants to get a quick podcast episode in."

That woke her up. "On my way!" she shouted.

It wasn't hard to convince my mother. She understood that the day was going to be kind of crazy. Kendra arrived, and I started out the door to meet her, but then stopped—I couldn't remember if I'd turned off the stove.

I ran back inside and thankfully found that it was off. On my way back to the door, I heard my mom at the top of the stairs.

I jogged up there, curious. "Mom?"

She jumped. "I thought you were gone."

"I'm leaving now. What are you doing?"

"Oh, just changing the vacuum cleaner bag."

"Up here?"

"Storm, I thought you had to hurry."

"I do," I said as I backed down the stairs. "See you later."

I went outside and closed the door behind me, pausing there for a moment, puzzled, before I tossed my things into Kendra's truck and climbed in.

"What's wrong," asked Kendra?

"Nothing. Hey, Mr. J."

"Good morning, Storm," he replied.

"Give me one of those bags," she said, reaching for the garment bag in the backseat.

We arrived at the school just as Raine was coming up the walk. There were a lot of cars already there, probably people setting up and testing things for graduation.

"See you at graduation," said Mr. J as we hopped out of the truck. I gave him a thumbs-up and we hurried inside the school.

Raine noticed that something was off with me immediately. He nudged me and whispered, "What's wrong?"

"It's nothing," I lied. I was tired and concerned about Teresa's "retribution," but it was more than that.

He gave me a knowing look but didn't press further. As soon as we walked into the room, he stopped me. I glanced up at him, and he kissed me gently on the lips.

Kendra screamed.

"I didn't think I handled that well the other night. I mean with the first kiss," he said.

"Wait, what? What first kiss? Storm?"

I shook my head, snapping out of gaga land. "Later," I told her. "We have to do this quickly." I opened my laptop and found the email announcing my DNA results were now available.

Raine came around the table. "Log in. Let's see if I'm right about Portugal and Greece."

"You said Scotland."

"Same difference."

I chuckled. "No, it's not."

"I'm the bad boy, Raine . . ." he began.

"And I'm the good girl . . ." I suddenly paused. How good was I? I didn't feel so good anymore. Not sense what happened to Teresa. I was a fraud.

"Storm, has there been a glitch in your programming?"

"Oh, sorry. Ha! A lot on my mind."

"No, we get it. If you attend Beacon High, you know what we're dealing with—the passing of a beloved classmate."

I lowered my head. "Okay, let's do this."

"Yeah, we're only a couple hours from graduation, so let's make this happen. Just a reminder of what we're doing—Storm's got her DNA results!"

An air horn sounded.

I clicked on the site and got the feeling that Rick zoomed the camera in on me.

"Here it comes, folks," said Raine. "The info we've been waiting on. Storm will finally know something about her background. It's all you, Storm."

The site showed an image of the whole globe. Once the results loaded, it would zoom in on the areas that were part of my heritage and show what percentage of me was from each country. Honestly, I didn't even try to guess while I waited for the results. I was just happy that I'd finally know where I came from.

Raine and I leaned into the screen. "I—I don't know if I'm reading this right. What is it saying?" I asked, then glanced at Raine.

His mouth dropped open, and he quickly made a cutting motion with his hand, signaling to stop the camera.

Right there in front of Raine, Kendra, and Rick . . . I think a part of me died.

33

R ick nodded at Raine and took over the podcast from the soundboard, trying to lighten the mood while we figured out the results. "They are too caught up in this. As they decipher the code, can we just talk about this new horror flick about cell phones? I'm scared to use mine now. That is not okay."

Raine read the results in a hushed tone as Kendra came over and stood behind us. "28% Nigeria, 12% Ivory Coast, 5% Cameroon, 25% England and Northwestern Europe, 17% Wales, and 13% Ireland." His voice trailed off.

My breath quickened. "What does that mean? What's going on?"

Raine ran a hand over his face and then stared at me as if he were looking for the answer to some mystery in my face.

Kendra's mouth hung open.

Raine sighed heavily and leaned back in his chair. "Crap."

"What?"

"Storm. You're Black."

"What?"

"You're mixed, like me. Biracial. You said you've never even seen a photo of your father, right? He was Black. Look there," he said and pointed. "They separated your DNA into parent one and parent two, showing what you got from each. All of your African DNA came from parent two. That's your father."

I sat there, stunned, struggling to process his words. Although I understood the results as soon as I read them, I just needed someone else to say it out loud.

Black? Me? I glanced over at Kendra again, who was still gaping at the screen.

"But my mom . . . she—she—she would have told me." I stammered and stood.

Raine placed a hand on my shoulder. "Maybe there's more to the story," he suggested gently.

I thought back to all the times I had asked my mom about my father over the years. She'd always avoided the question or changed the subject. She had been hiding the truth from me for my whole life.

"Why wouldn't she tell me?" I whispered. Tears began to well up in my eyes. This revelation turned my whole sense of identity upside down. I was a stranger in my own skin.

Raine pulled me into a hug. "I can't answer that, Storm. But at least now you know who you are."

I clung to him, taking deep breaths to calm myself down. I knew Raine meant well, but how could I know who I was when I didn't know my father's family? They were out there somewhere.

I pulled away and wiped my eyes, while Kendra just continued to stare at me. "Say something," I told her.

"I . . . I don't know what to say," she admitted. "This is huge."

"But . . ."

"You have to admit, I already called it."

"Yeah," I replied, remembering when she said I could be mixed like Mariah Carey. I looked back at the screen, at the definitive proof of my African heritage. "I have to talk to my mother, like right now."

I grabbed my laptop and dashed out of the door with Kendra and Raine following closely behind.

"Storm, slow down!" Kendra screamed.

I kept running, through the library, down the hall, and out of the school, ignoring everything else except the road leading to my house. Though I saw our car was gone, I ran into the house, screaming for my mother. I tore into the kitchen, looked out the window to the backyard, and ran up the stairs to her bedroom. She was definitely gone.

I set my laptop on her bed, opened her closet and pulled down the gun safe. I pushed past my friends, got the key from her medicine cabinet, and went back and opened the box.

"What are you doing?" asked Kendra. She and Raine stood over me while I squatted, pulling everything out of the box.

"Open these," I told them and tossed envelopes in their direction.

"But this is someone else's mail," said Kendra.

"Forget it, I'll do it." I started opening the ones on the bottom. Kendra and Raine glanced at each other and reluctantly opened the ones on the floor.

"They are all apologies from some Clarence guy," said Raine.

"Storm, how did you know about these? Who is he? Is this about your father?" Kendra paused. "What is that?"

I held up a ring I found at the bottom of the box. It looked like an antique, and it needed to be cleaned. The diamond was pear-shaped and yellow.

My mind immediately flashed to what I read in one of the letters: *Enclosed is a key to a safe deposit box at First National Bank on Main Street. Leave it inside. Please. It will change everything.*

The letter was talking about this ring. I stuffed it in my pocket.

"Storm?" my mother called, coming into the house. "You left the door wide open. Storm? I thought I wouldn't see you until you crossed the stage."

I stood and Raine grabbed me. He lowered his voice. "What if your mother doesn't know? What if your father was passing?"

"Passing for white? No. There are a whole lot of secrets in this house, and I'm going to find out what they are." I grabbed my laptop from the bed and bounded down the stairs with my friends following.

Kendra tried to stop me. "Just wait, Storm. Storm! Wait!"

"What are you doing here?" my mom asked as I came into the kitchen. She had already done her makeup for graduation. Pity. Her mascara and eyeliner were about to be a mess.

I set my laptop on the kitchen table and opened it. My head was spinning as the wifi connected and I pointed at the screen. "Is there something you'd like to tell me?"

Her smile faded into a straight line as she glanced past me at Kendra and Raine.

I told myself to calm down—that I had to be respectful and not yell at my mother. That she had a good explanation, and right now, I just needed to listen to her. "Mom . . ." I said softly and pointed at the screen. "These are my DNA results."

She moved closer to the table. "What are you talking about? You had your DNA tested without my consent?"

"What did you expect me to do when you wouldn't tell me anything about me—about us? Mom," I shook my head, "How could you not tell me?"

She didn't even look at the screen. Obviously, she didn't need to. "You won't understand this, but it was for your own good."

"For my own good? How could you only raise me as white? Why did you take everything away from me—my heritage, my culture?"

She put down the Starbucks cup she had been holding and reached for me.

"Don't touch me. I just want the truth. Please. I'm tired of your secrets. For once, just tell me the truth. All that I want is a yes or no answer. Did you purposely do this to me?"

"Yes," she admitted. "I did."

I clasped my stomach feeling like the wind had been knocked out of me. All of my life I wondered about my father, imagining someone who looked like me—someone with my light brown hair, which I'd always highlighted so that it looked as blonde as Mom's, someone with my complexion, much tanner than my mother's and my green eyes.

How had I never questioned why she and I looked so different?

"Why?" I asked, my voice shaking.

"It wasn't that I was purposefully keeping it from you. I just . . . I didn't know how to bring it up, I guess. Or when. I thought maybe when you were older we could have that conversation. But months passed, then years, and I didn't think about it. Then it seemed too late."

"But you let me believe . . ." I trailed off, not even sure what I believed anymore.

"I'm so sorry, honey," my mom said. "I should have told you. It was wrong of me to keep his identity from you."

Tears filled her eyes, but I felt nothing. I leaned over the table and copied the section on my DNA and pasted it into the open section of my paper so I could send it off to my teacher.

"What are you doing?"

I ignored the question and typed: *I'm Black and I am just finding out. There's nothing more to say. Now I'm going to try and find my family.*

My mother read the words before I clicked send. "Storm, don't. You can't."

My voice was firm. "Did my father really die?"

"Yes."

"Then who are those letters from in your fake gun safe?"

Her eyes widened.

"Please don't lie," I added.

Raine motioned to Kendra, and they backed away. I didn't know if they left, but they gave us privacy that I didn't care if we had.

My mother sat. "Okay . . . I guess it's time to tell you everything."

34

—　·　—

"Those letters . . ." She glanced at me with an understanding that I knew more than I let on.

"The red envelopes from Clarence." I replied.

"Yes. Clarence is my father. He has been looking for me for years and finally found me."

I thought for a moment. "Who was—Wait, was that man who was at the house when I came home a private investigator? I mean, he didn't look old enough to be your father."

She nodded. "I didn't lie about him. I did know him a long time ago. He found us once, some years ago. That's when you remember him from."

She paused and I waited for her to continue. She inhaled deeply.

"The reason my father didn't know where I was is because he disowned me when I married your father. He didn't want anything to do with a Black grandchild. Yes, things are different now, but in a small town like Beaufordville, not much had changed, despite what was happening out in the world."

She looked off to some faraway place above my head. "Clarence, your grandfather, was the only family I had after my mother and grandparents died. He loved me once, but not after I married your father. I was like you, Stormie. I was a good girl and had done everything I could, trying to be perfect, to make my father happy, because he was a hard man.

"He didn't care for me leaving the family and going off to the military after high school. But that was one of the reasons I did it—to get away from my family."

"And that's where you met my father?"

Her gaze fell on me and brightened, as if just seeing her newborn baby. She held a slight grin. "I met your father before that. We planned to go to the military together. We had it all figured out." Her smile faded. "We got married at nineteen. The next year, I witnessed your father's vehicle blow up in front of mine in Iraq. Shortly after that, I found out I was pregnant. My tour was over. I was released from active duty and returned to civilian life. So, I came home. My father welcomed me and were happy about my pregnancy . . . until they found out my husband was Black. By that time, I was showing—my belly was huge. It didn't matter. He father picked me up, carried me outside, and dropped me on the ground."

I gasped.

My mother wiped her eyes. "'You will never step foot in this house again. Don't come back here!' he yelled. I could have miscarried. He didn't care. I crawled to the end of the walk until I could pull myself up by the old wooden fence post. I can still fill the shards piercing my hand." She sniffed. "I made it to my car. But, when I left that day, I was in agreement with my father. I vowed never to go back to that house, nor see him again.

"Despite the fall, you made it here, healthy. But you didn't come out looking like your father at all. You never did get his caramel skin or hair texture. I praised God because I thought he was trying to help me hide you. If my father wanted to find me, he wouldn't look for a white woman with a white baby with green eyes and blonde hair. So I didn't even tell the hospital you were biracial."

"But I don't understand. Why did you think he would bother to look for you?"

"Because he blamed me for my mother's death."

35

— • —

Kendra cleared her throat. "Storm, if you're going to walk with your graduating class, we have to get to the school. You're going to be late," she said from the living room. I guess she had waited until there was a pause in our conversation.

I hadn't even realized she was still there. I looked behind her, expecting to see Raine, but he wasn't there.

"You didn't come this far for nothing. Go. We can finish this discussion later," said my mother.

I nodded and stood, not expecting my legs to tremble as if I were afraid. "Maybe then you will explain your reasoning for trying to keep me sick."

Her mouth opened, but I held a hand up. "Don't. I think I figured it out. It's the reason I never get sick at Kendra's house. I know I have asthma, but I think you've made it worse to keep me here. You don't want me going off to college because it's always been just the two of us, but you wanted me to be the one to make the decision. That's why you had the vacuum cleaner bag open. You've been putting the dust around the house, right?"

Kendra gasped.

I marched out of the kitchen, and Kendra followed me through the living room.

I didn't care nearly as much about graduating as I had that morning. Nothing mattered anymore. But one thing was for sure: I'd rather be at Beacon High with half the senior body hating me than in my house with my mother. Maybe I would feel different later, but for now, I didn't want to be around her.

I stopped at the front door and turned back to my mother. "You know that recurring dream I've been having about the world ending?"

She only looked at me.

"It was right. Did you notice the date? It wasn't everyone's world that was ending. Just mine."

Her hand sprang up to her mouth as she fought back tears.

As I turned away, I noticed the ticker at the bottom of the television screen. No one had to tell me it was coming; I felt it inside me. A tropical storm was moving through the panhandle, and though it was supposed to steer clear of us, I knew I was drawing it near.

"Raine had to go and get ready," Kendra told me once we were outside.

I understood. It wasn't his problem anyway.

"Why didn't you tell me about all of this going on? This explains your behavior lately."

"It was complicated." My eyes widened. "Was the podcast live or just recorded?"

"Don't worry, Raine took care of that. It was recorded, but he had Rick delete it. That's not the way for everyone to find out. I mean, if you want people to find out."

I gave it some thought. "Why not? It's who I am, whether I look like it or not. You know what? It kind of feels good to know something about my life, even though I was lied to about it for so long."

"Don't hate your mother, Storm. I mean, what she's done is crazy. But think about it this way: God chose her to bring you into this world. Now it's up to you to decide where your relationship goes from here."

"I don't hate her. I just don't like her right now. I'm so disappointed in—" My words caught in my throat, and I fell silent. If I broke down right then, I would never make it to graduation, so I forced back the pain.

We went back to the recording studio in the library and got my things. Kendra helped me get ready in the bathroom. I took the ring I found in the box in my mother's closet and slipped it on the gold chain around my neck. Kendra brushed my hair, and her eyes watered as she handed me my cap and gown. "I'm sorry," she said as she wiped her eyes. "Reality is setting in that you won't be here with me next year. Why can't I be smart like you?"

"Ken, you're the smartest person I know. Besides, you're going to rule the school next year. And I can't believe you have a boyfriend before me."

She sniffed. "Yeah, Bryson is pretty great. But after what I saw, I think we both have boyfriends now. We can double."

I grinned at her, and she watched me in the mirror as I put my cap on.

"I'll be in the stands with your mom, if she still comes, and my dad—near the center, screaming as loud as I can."

She hugged me hard. I didn't realize how much I needed a hug until that moment and squeezed her just as hard.

"It's going to be okay, Stormie."

I wiped my eyes and nodded. If I said anything, then I would really start bawling.

36

"Will the audience please rise for the procession of graduates," Principal Stanton announced.

The band played and the audience cheered as the Beacon High senior class walked out onto the football field in single file, I wondered who would clap for me when my name was called. I'd be shocked if I got even one "Whew! Stormie!" from my classmates. Before I slapped Pool, I may have gotten a louder applause than anyone.

But I didn't need their validation. Soon, this day would fade like a whisper.

We lined up in front of our seats and stood until we were given the signal to sit. We were seated at the center of the football field with no shade or covering. It was the warmest day of the year thus far, and I patted my pocket, making sure I hadn't forgotten my inhaler. I was glad the graduation was early in the day before the air became too thick.

The stands quickly filled up to the left and right of us, mostly on the home team side, which still had some shade.

Some people were smart and brought umbrellas, while others held flowers and balloons. Eventually, the home team side filled, and the latecomers were ushered to the visitor side where they sat in full sun.

I just wanted it all to be over quickly so I could determine what course my life would take moving forward. *Just toss my diploma at me already and let me go,* I grumbled to myself.

"To the parents, grandparents, family members, and friends of our graduates, we appreciate your presence at this important event. Today's ceremony is a significant milestone as we celebrate the achievements of our students. As this is a formal occasion, we ask everyone to maintain a respectful atmosphere, allowing each graduate to be properly recognized as we honor the Beacon High School class of 2025!"

The audience cheered, and something caught my eye. To my right, a red star-shaped balloon escaped from someone in the stands and flew high over the twelve rows of the graduating class of Beacon High.

1. *Red balloon*

The notes from Teresa's notebook flashed through my mind (the signal to get everything started), along with my dream about the end of the world. I shot up, the only graduate standing, and looked around, my heart racing.

"What are you doing?" Deanna, the girl to my right asked. Her brow furrowed in confusion. Laughter rippled from the graduates behind me, and the teacher at the end of my row motioned for me to sit down.

I sat again. *That was just a coincidence. They're not possibly going through with this.*

I closed my eyes and breathed as deeply as I could. We sat there, sweating profusely from either the sun's rays beating down on the right side of our faces or nervousness, in our black robes and caps with yellow tassels hanging on the right.

When I opened my eyes again, I smiled up at the balloon as it floated higher. It was escaping—something I longed for and would be doing in September when I started college in Florida. Then I could put all of this behind me and become the real me.

The teacher motioned for my row, the honor students, to stand. We rose and followed her. I stopped at the twenty-yard line between the 2 and the 0, waiting for my name to be called.

"Graduating with honors," Mrs. Fisher said from the podium beside the stage, "Deanna Bevica Monroe." She was the girl before me. She did a shimmy, as everyone cheered, and headed up the stairs. Someone in her family screamed her name from the bleachers.

I wondered why we had to give middle names. I didn't like mine at all. *Lynn* just didn't sound like a cute name to me. It was better than Bevica, though.

Mrs. Fisher announced that Deanna was graduating from high school with an associate degree, just like I was. I eyed her flats with envy as she climbed the steps and skipped effortlessly across the stage. You'd never guess that someone as smart as me showed up in heels I could barely walk in just because I liked the bling on them.

Next in line, I stepped forward and handed my index card to Mrs. Fisher. She smiled at me, and even though she knew my name, she glanced at the card before announcing it.

I looked up at the sky and imagined how my classmates would have looked at me if at that very moment, a plane flew overhead and circled, pulling my name behind it, everyone reading in their heads: *Happy Graduation, Stormie! Yeah, that would be epic.*

But what I actually saw sent prickles up my spine. The most massive cloud was blowing in, enveloping the area in a gray filter.

2. The sky cries

Again, it had to be a coincidence.

I looked ahead of me at the steps that led up to the stage I would have to climb to shake Principal Stanton's hand. I had it down pat. There was no way I'd make a mistake, unless I tripped like I almost did on the way to my seat.

Shake his hand, pause for a photo, shake more hands, walk down the steps on the other side of the stage. You can do this, I told myself. *Armpits, stop sweating already.*

I glanced over at the seniors that were still seated and noticed Pool's friends glaring at me as if their eyes would cause me to melt and disappear.

Suddenly, the balloon that should have floated away by then hovered above the stage. Then something slammed into it, deflating it and sending it crashing into the podium with force.

Someone screamed as hail pounded the football field and tornado sirens blared over the graduation ceremony.

Is this possible? I asked myself, remembering my dream: *The heavens weep* and Teresa's notes: *The sky cries.*

37

— · —

"**T**his way! This way!" school staff and security offi-cers yelled. They ushered us inside the school to the auditorium. The graduating class was directed to the bottom floor, seated in the same order as on the field, and the visitors up to the balcony—parents, grandparents, and siblings only. There wasn't enough room for anyone else.

Principal Stanton took his place at the podium. "Let's get this going so we can get you home. It seems that we are going to see a bit of this storm after all."

Those of us who were standing on the field stood in the aisle to the right of the stage, and I was at the front. From my place in line, I glanced back and noticed Rick leaving the auditorium. The boy with the short dreadlocks followed him.

My breathing quickened. *What's next? Uh . . . Uh . . . Gravity falls—but what does that mean?* My eyes met Raine's, but auditorium lights shut off. There were a few panicked yelps from the audience. But as quickly as they'd shut off, they flickered back on.

"Maybe we should postpone this," said Principal Stanton with a nervous chuckle.

"No!" the senior class collectively yelled.

"Okay, okay. You've waited a long time for this, so I understand how anxious you are to get this done today. As Mrs. Fisher calls your name, come up. We are not going to stop between students, so keep the line flowing," said Principal Stanton.

What was supposed to happen next? Worms. I glanced around the ground expecting to see them writhing everywhere.

"Storm Davis," Mrs. Fisher called.

Did she just call me?

The boy behind me tapped my shoulder and pointed. "That's the second time she's said your name."

I was about to take a step forward, but a screen began to lower from above the stage. Principal Stanton glanced behind him. As soon as the screen got to the floor, Teresa's image appeared.

Murmurs came from the audience.

"Due to the weather, we will not have time for tributes today," said the principal.

Suddenly, Teresa's voice rang out from the speakers. "This is what happened to me." The once vibrant girl now appeared fragile in the next slide, and her voice trembled as she spoke.

"Who's doing this?" asked the principal. His mouth continued to move, but his mic shut off.

The image captured Teresa's tear-stained face, and a montage unfolded, each frame a testament to the relentless cruelty inflicted upon her.

In one scene, Teresa sat alone in the school cafeteria, her tray untouched, as whispers and mocking laughter swirled around her like a suffocating fog. The next video revealed her shaking hands clutching her textbooks as she walked the hallways—her steps hesitant, as if expecting an attack at any moment. Graffiti stained her gym locker, cruel words covering it from top to bottom in bold letters.

Then, the screen displayed a series of text messages, each one more venomous than the last.

You're worthless.

Nobody likes you.

Why don't you just kill yourself?

Teresa's voice grew stronger. "They tore me down, piece by piece. But I refused to let them get away with it." She paused, as if letting it all soak in for a moment. "Pool tried to kill me."

He shot out of his seat. "What? I did not. Who is that? Who's doing this?"

"And he's done things to others. They're just too afraid to admit it."

"Stop this, now!" yelled a man from the balcony that I assumed was Pool's father. "How dare you!"

My eyes scanned the auditorium. Pool's friends looked afraid, some of my classmates looked shocked, others looked mournful. None of the staff moved or said a word.

"You owe me," echoed in my head, and I took a step up to the stage. Slowly, at first, and then I was at the podium as everyone looked at me.

Pool shook his head.

I slipped out of my shoes. If I was going to do this, I was going to be stable. "It's not a lie. I saw what you and Tiffany Lancaster did to Teresa. I was at the carnival right in front of you."

Pool charged over the auditorium seats to the aisle. But before he could reach the stage, Todd sprang from his seat and tackled him, sending both boys sprawling onto the carpeted floor. They wrestled, fists flying as they rolled. Pool landed a solid punch, knocking Todd back before clawing his way forward, eyes locked on the stage. Despite several students trying to hold him back, Pool shoved and tore through their grip forcing his way to me.

Everyone was getting out of the way while the security team tried to reach him.

Behind me, something was happening.

The entire senior class was pointing, clasping their hands over their mouths, gasping and screaming, and from what I could see, a few fainted.

Pool stopped dead in his tracks.

I slowly turned. Teresa stood in front of the curtain, in white, looking like a ghost. I stumbled back a few steps. *Return from the dead.*

Raine ran toward me and screamed something. I couldn't hear him over the commotion of people fleeing in every direction, terrified. He lifted his hand in my direction, and I grabbed my shoes and ran to him. I jumped off the stage and into his arms and we ran with everyone else, pushing through the crowd and out of the building.

Everything was so quiet and still outside. I knelt, slipping on my heels, and looking up at the sky. If there was one thing I was certain of, it was weather—this was a tornado sky.

Then, I noticed a huge wall cloud south of us.

"Come on!" yelled Raine as he hopped on his motorcycle. I climbed on behind him, and we shot off down the street. I held on tight, pressing the side of my head against his back.

When he finally stopped, we were at a highway truck stop. Just as he shut off the engine, a car door slammed behind us, and I spun around.

"Kendra?"

"I hightailed it out of there right behind you."

"But you took your dad's truck," I said as we hugged.

"Yeah."

"And you don't have a license," I whispered.

"Nope."

"You're going to be grounded for life."

She shrugged. "He'll get over it. He was busy running your mom to safety when he dropped his keys."

Bryson, Rick, and a girl I barely knew named Lonnie hopped out of the other doors.

I followed Raine inside to a booth, and the others followed me. "Why are we here?" I asked him.

"I don't know. I was trying to get us as far away from whatever that was as I could and just headed north."

My phone vibrated in my pocket, but I didn't check it.

The server came over with a huge smile, revealing her braces. "Well, looka here. We've got graduates in caps and gowns. What would you like for breakfast on this beautiful morning?"

"Can you give us a minute?" asked Raine.

She snapped her gum and looked at us oddly. "Sure, honey."

"So . . . What *was* that? Teresa's not dead?" asked Lonnie. "I certainly wasn't sticking around to see if that was an apparition. No one's making me part of some horror story."

Everyone looked at me and waited, as if I had all the answers.

"I thought she was," I told them. "But I also know there were things she wanted to happen at graduation."

"She's not," said Rick. "I was part of the task force she put together to orchestrate her plan to get Pool and the rest of them back upon her fake death. Her parents were in on it. They wanted to teach them a lesson, no matter the cost. It didn't all play out as it was planned because of the weather."

"But the balloon," I said.

"We shot it down."

Raine motioned with a finger. "How did you all end up—"

"I was looking for Kendra," said Bryson.

"Yeah, we're dating. I was like an Olympic sprinter getting up out of there."

"I got chased from the sound room by security. I ran to the first vehicle that had a clearing out of there," said Rick.

"I was just running," said Lonnie, "and hopped in too. Do you all realize we just left our parents?"

"What else could we do? They were nowhere near us, and everyone ran in different directions."

"Oh no, your grandmother," I told Raine.

"She's fine. She's in town, but she stayed at my house because of the weather alert. My sister is with her."

"Good, because I think we may have dodged a tornado."

"She would know," said Kendra.

"Well, what now, graduates—and Kendra?" asked Raine.

I pulled my phone from my pocket. "I need to get to this address."

Kendra squinted at the screen. "Beaufordville?"

"You can read that writing?" I asked

"Yeah. Where's Beaufordville?"

"Beaufordville?" repeated the server, coming back to our table. "You're not far. It's only about twenty minutes northwest of here."

Kendra held up her keys. "I can drive."

"All of us?" I asked.

"Well, we're all here."

"This wasn't exactly how I planned to spend graduation day, but it's the most excitement I've had all year, so I'm in," said Lonnie.

"What about the weather?" asked Kendra.

"I'm going regardless. I have to."

"Why?"

I didn't look at anyone. I stared at the ice in the cup in front of me, then watched the raindrops dripping down the window. "I got my DNA results."

"Oh, yeah," said Lonnie. "I wondered when that would happen. I was curious about it. What did you find out?"

"I found out that . . . I'm Black."

"Excuse me?" said Bryson.

"You heard her," said Kendra.

"You mean you didn't know?"

I shook my head. I still didn't look up, knowing they were staring at me."

"I mean, I can kind of see it now," said Bryson.

"You only see it because she told you."

"No, I see it too. It's why I thought Portugal or Spain would be in your ancestry," said Raine. "So what is the address to?"

"The grandfather I didn't know I had."

38

We all climbed inside Kendra's father's truck and drove in silence. Raine sat beside me in the front seat, his fingers entwined with mine. It was comforting, and warmth enveloped me, relieving some of the numbness I felt.

The J's Empanadas pickup truck sped down the highway as the rain finally stopped. It made sense—I was calming down.

"This is the exit, coming up," said Bryson, navigating from the back seat.

Kendra swerved in front of the car that had been in her blind spot and pulled off the highway as we all screamed.

"Kendra, do you even have a license?" asked Rick.

"Nope. But I think it would've made sense for you to ask that before you got in the car with me, don't you think? Anyway, no one else is driving my father's truck but me. Okay, where do I go? Where do I go?" she repeated as the light turned green.

"Oh, turn right, then left at the next light. Keep going until I tell you to turn again," Bryson said, following a map app on his phone.

Finally, we pulled in front of a house with an old white wooden fence. I stared at it, wondering if the posts was the same ones my mother used to pull herself up after her father dropped her.

"This is the place," I said.

"How do you know? You've never been there before," Kendra asked.

"Trust me. It is."

"Eww, there are cicadas all over the fence," said Lonnie.

"It's that time of year," Rick replied.

We must have sat there for about five minutes, staring at the house, before Raine finally asked, "Are you sure you want to do this?"

I nodded, and he opened the car door and let me out of the front seat.

I walked through the opening between the two sides of the fence and up to the front door. I stood there a moment before I knocked on the screen door. The door behind it was open.

"Who's there?"

I didn't know what to say. It was not like he would know me. Finally, I said, "It's Storm."

The door creaked fully open, and a figure stood behind the screen.

He stepped closer, and beneath his drooping eyelids were green eyes.

My green eyes.

It was him . . . My grandfather.

He brushed his short white hair back over his forehead, as though it were long enough to fall into his eyes, then stared at the ring hanging from the chain around my neck.

"A red envelope."

He opened the screen and stepped out onto the porch. With each step that he took forward, I took a step back.

He looked up and down the block. "Where is—Are you alone?"

"I am. I wanted to visit you. I—I thought I could stay for a while."

He turned to go back inside the house. "You shouldn't be here."

"Are you going to do the same thing to me that you did to her?"

He stopped walking.

"She told me everything." I didn't expect to cry, but tears streamed down my cheeks. "We needed you. You have no idea what we've been through."

"Is everything all right over there, Clarence?" a neighbor called from the other side of a hedge of viburnum.

He held a hand up to her.

I continued as if I didn't even hear her. "I'm a good girl. You would be proud of me." I pointed at my robe. "I even graduated today, a year early."

A car door slammed. "Storm, are you okay?" Raine asked, running up to us.

From behind me, he demanded from Clarence, "Why is she crying? What did you say to her?"

I motioned for him to calm down.

"We don't have much time," I told Clarence. "We need to make things right before . . ."

"Before what?" he asked.

A siren blared, and a white Dodge Charger screeched to a halt in front of the house. Bold gold letters outlined in black spelled out "County Sheriff." The driver's door swung open, and a sheriff's deputy stepped out.

"Good afternoon, Clarence."

"Afternoon, John."

"We received a call about a strange black truck sitting in front of your house and someone said they heard screaming. I'm here to investigate and ensure everyone's safety."

"That girl right there," said the neighbor.

"Me?"

"She didn't do anything," said Raine.

"I think she's the one who broke into my car last week. It's the same hair on my doorbell camera."

"No, it wasn't me. I just came to town."

"Miss, I'm going to have to take you in for questioning."

"You're arresting me?"

"Don't touch her," said Raine. "You have no right."

My friends jumped out of the truck, phones in hand, capturing every second of the scene. Their voices rose in a mix of panic and anger, yelling at the officer as they stepped closer, desperate to document what was happening.

Raine tried to step between us.

The officer placed his hand on his pistol. "Son, back up."

I pulled out my phone, filming it also.

"Put the phone down," the officer said.

"We didn't do anything," I told him as he grabbed me.

"Take your hands off my granddaughter."

39

Clarence's voice sliced through the air, and he stepped off the porch.

The officer let go of my arm, and I lowered my phone and turned to my grandfather, my heart pounding in sync with the thrumming cicadas.

"Your granddaughter, Clarence?" asked the officer. Why didn't you say so?"

"John, look at them. They're all wearing graduation robes. Well, except for one. Did you really think they were up to no good?"

"Storm!" my mother yelled. I turned to see her and Kendra's father jump out of Betty and rush toward us.

Clarence's eyes widened as she approached. Tears filled his eyes and hers. They stood a few feet apart.

"Is there a problem, officer?" my mom asked.

He glanced at Clarence. "No ma'am, not anymore. Enjoy your visit."

"You!" Mr. J said, pointing at Kendra. "Give me my keys!" Then he said a few things in Spanish to her that I didn't understand.

"But dad," Kendra replied and sulked.

"How did you find me?" I asked my mom.

"We waited at the school. When we didn't find either of you and saw that the truck was gone, I knew you would be here." She turned back to her father.

"Let's take this inside," he said, looking around at the neighbors in their yards.

My friends followed us. The house looked like nothing had been redecorated since maybe the '80s. It was clean, just old.

Clarence looked around at everyone. "Maybe they should—"

I shook my head. "They know everything. It's okay if they hear this."

My mother gasped, placing a hand over her chest as she turned in a circle, looking at the furniture and the pictures on the walls. "Nothing has changed here; it's exactly the same. Well, except for the television."

She picked up a photo of a woman holding a toddler, framed in wood, stared at it for a moment, then set it down again with a soft whimper. "I didn't get to tell you the whole story before you left, Stormie. And you were right about everything. The—the dust too. I'm so sorry. I hope you don't hate me."

"I just want to know the truth. All of it."

"Your father and I fell in love and were secretly dating. We planned to get married, but he didn't have a ring." She lifted the ring on the chain around my neck. "He took his mother's ring. When his parents couldn't find it, they blamed the maid at the hotel they were staying at for their anniversary. That maid was my mother."

Clarence listened and turned away.

"My mother was arrested. Your father was ashamed and never told the truth. We thought they would hate him if he did. I didn't want my parents to hate the man I was going to marry. My mother was never the same after she was released from jail, because of how harshly she was treated." My mom's voice trailed off.

Clarence finished where she left off. "They went off to the military together, married there, and she came home pregnant. I was so happy to see my daughter, but then I saw she was wearing that ring. The same ring from the photos during the trial. At that moment, I saw red—I knew one of them had taken the ring. That's why she was kicked out."

A heavy silence hung in the air. I couldn't believe what I was hearing. "So you didn't kick her out because her husband was Black?" I asked.

"No!" Clarence exclaimed. "After what they did to my wife, when all they had to do was tell the truth . . . And to think they had the ring the whole time. I wanted nothing to do with her. I figured she had a choice: tell the truth about her boyfriend and protect her mother, or stay loyal to him without caring what might happen to her mother. Write or wrong, I can tell you this . . . I've always regretted the way I put Rebecca out."

"You have to believe me. We didn't think it would go that far. The authorities had no proof that my mother took the ring. It should have all blown over." My mother's eyes were wet with tears as she looked at me. "We were young and foolish, Storm. We didn't think about the consequences of our actions, and we were scared of what might happen if we told the truth."

"That's how children think," Clarence interjected. "It killed my wife."

I realized that my mother must have put the ring in that box soon after she left her parent's house that day. That's why I never saw it before.

"Wait, so Storm is . . ." Mr. J began.

"Storm is mixed," Kendra finished.

He stared at my mother, speechless.

I unlatched the necklace and held it out to Clarence. "You wanted this. Here. Take it."

His trembling hand reached for the ring, closing around it in a tight fist without even looking at it.

Though the story explained so much, it was still hard to grasp that over a decade of pain and estrangement had stemmed from a simple lie told so long ago. "I wish you had told the truth back then," I said quietly. "Maybe things could have been different. You can't undo the past, but this has gone on for far too long. Even if you don't want to be in each other's lives from this point on, you need to forgive each other."

I pushed my mom toward Clarence. They looked into each other's eyes, then nodded. Clarence reached for her and pulled her into his arms. They both cried.

Immediately a weight lifted, not only from them and the quaint room, but the world outside; the skies grew brighter, and the sun shone through the windows.

"Storm," said my mom, wiping her eyes, "this is your grandfather, Clarence."

"Hello," I said, as if I hadn't just met him. "I have your eyes."

He smiled through his tears. "I noticed that right away."

"And this is her best friend, Kendra, and their friends. And this is Kendra's father, Julius."

Everyone grinned and said hello.

Raine clasped my hand, and I thought of my dream. The date of the world's end became less important than the impact we could have in the time we have on this earth.

Suddenly, the sharp blare of a horn cut through the air, and we all froze, exchanging puzzled glances. We looked around us for the source. Then, in the blink of an eye, Kendra vanished. Her jeans, T-shirt, and sneakers crumpled to the ground where she had been standing. One by one, my friends disappeared, leaving nothing but heaps of clothes scattered across the floor.

I looked back at my mom, and she reached for me.

Then, in an instant, I disappeared.

Matthew 24:36 But of that day and hour no one knows, not even the angels of heaven, but My Father only.

What will you do with the time you have?

Please Leave A Review

Your review means the world to me. I greatly appreciate any kind words. Even one or two sentences go a long way in helping readers discover *What the Good Girl Knew*. Thank you in advance.

Don't Miss Out!

Exclusive content, discounts, and giveaways are available only to L. B. Anne's VIP members. Use the link below to sign up. There is no charge or obligation.

www.lbanne.com/vip-club

ABOUT AUTHOR

L. B. Anne is best known for her Christian middle grade, Sheena Meyer, series about a girl with a special gift and a destiny that can save the world. L. B. Anne lives on the Gulf Coast of Florida with her husband and is a full-time author, coach, and mental health advocate. When she's not inventing new obstacles for her diverse characters to overcome, you can find her reading, playing bass guitar, running on the beach, or downing a mocha iced coffee at a local cafe while dreaming of being your favorite author. Visit L. B. at www.lbanne.com

Instagram: Instagram.com/authorlbanne

Facebook: Facebook.com/authorlbanne

Twitter: twitter.com/authorlbanne

Pinterest: pinterest.com/AuthorLBAnne